Jonas felt scared and alone...

"*It's not fair,* he thought as he lay in bed, examining the ring by the moonlight. No one understands.

I do. The voice whispered from a shadowy corner in the room. *And I'm the only one you need. You saw it. We are invincible.*

'Yeah.' Jonas nodded and slipped the ring onto his finger.

Sleep well, the voice said. *Tomorrow we will show them all.*"

ALSO AVAILABLE:

BOOK 1

The adventure begins when Jonas Shurmann teams up with cat detectives, CatBob and Neil Higgins, to investigate a wave of feline disappearances in their neighborhood in *Missing*.

BOOK 2

The adventure continues as Jonas Shurmann and his partners, CatBob and Neil Higgins, race to break a hundred year old curse before it ruins Orville Dusenbury's life in *The Dusenbury Curse*.

To Ava, the power is within you!

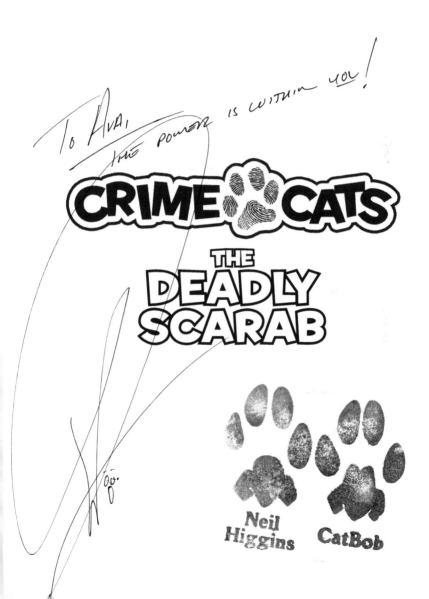

CRIME CATS

THE DEADLY SCARAB

Neil Higgins   **CatBob**

THE DEADLY SCARAB

WRITTEN & ILLUSTRATED BY **WOLFGANG PARKER**

EDITED BY **BEN SOSTROM**

I would like to express my gratitude to the following friends. Their contributions and support have made this book possible.

Kitty Maer, Ben Sostrom, Doug Clay, Ross Hughes, Alycia Yates, Gail Harbert and Cat Welfare of Ohio Association, Jamison Pack, Jodie Engle, Tricia Yanscik, Geoffrey Bachert, Joan Harless, Vinnie "Mad Chain" Maneri, Regan and Jonas Tonti, my retail partners, and the cats of Clintonville and their wonderful families.

Special thanks to Nia Johnson, Sarah Dearth, and Laura Douglass for graciously allowing me to use their invention, "Fish-Girl and Meows," in this book.

CRIME CATS: THE DEADLY SCARAB
RL 4. 008—012

To Clintonville:

For all that you are and all that I dream you to be. Thank you for rescuing me.

~ W.P.

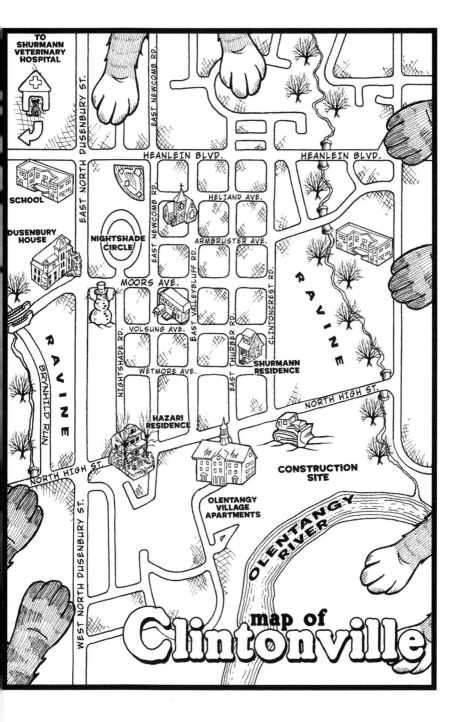

PROLOGUE

Tick-tick-tick!

Corwin Bachert gently turned the dial to the left, paused, then twisted it back right.

Tick-tick-tick!

He grimaced as he gripped the handle and carefully pulled it down. The lock responded with a crisp *click!* The door swung open and Corwin pulled a small wooden box from the compartment.

"Move it, Slim," he called down to the handsome tuxedo cat circling his feet. "We don't want to drop this."

Slim trotted beside him, sniffing the air and eyeing the box.

Corwin carefully placed his cargo on a small desk in the center of the room and straightened up. Slim leaped up to investigate the prize, but Corwin snatched him up and sat him on the couch.

"No, no, no, Slim," he scolded. "You might think that box is full of treats, but it's not. Believe me, you don't want what's in there." He pointed to the bed beyond an archway, where a pair of eyes glowed in the gloom under the bed frame. "See, Trash has the right idea. You need to go hide under the bed with him until I'm done." He nudged Slim with his foot, but the feline stood his ground and meowed in protest.

Corwin peeled off the rubber gloves he'd been wearing and replaced them with a fresh pair. Then he took up a camera and snapped a few shots. The box was only about six inches wide and Corwin had to lean in to capture all of the faded details weather and time had tried to erase from its surface. Then Corwin carefully gripped the lid and pulled it back.

Inside a beetle lay nestled in a scrap of velvet fabric that was blotted with brownish stains. The insect was made of polished stone and affixed to a crudely crafted band. It was a ring.

Corwin gazed down at the artifact as if he expected it to leap from the box and bite him. He took up his camera and snapped a few more shots. After a quick review of the images he set the camera aside and plucked the beetle from its nest. He turned it this way and that, scrutinizing it through his bifocals.

The craftsmanship was exquisite. Corwin had never seen anything like it.

Suddenly a loud crash rang through the house. Corwin started and turned toward the stairwell, straining his ears for a clue to the cause. But the throb of his quickened pulse was all he could hear.

He turned his attention back to the ring just in time to catch the beetle's wings snap open. One of stone wedges sliced into the tip of his finger. Corwin yelped and placed the item back in its box, then clenched the damaged glove in his teeth and pulled his hand free. As he pressed a fresh tissue to the wound, he watched the blood he had left on the polished wing collect and drip onto its velvet nest. The beetle had added another stain to its collection.

A second crash came from downstairs. Corwin grabbed a wooden baseball bat from a brass umbrella stand and padded down the steps.

Corwin's antique shop occupied the ground floor, with only the staircase separating his living space from his business. He tiptoed to the bottom of the stairs and scanned the shop but he couldn't see anyone among the shelves and furniture.

"Who's there?" he called.

He carefully wound his way through the maze of merchandise and froze when he caught a wispy shadow out of the corner of his eye. He raised his bat but found no one there. A strange howling sound arose outside. Another shadow slithered behind an antique sofa. Corwin leaped to cut off its escape, but found nothing again.

The howling noise grew louder and clearer, as if the source of the sound was getting closer. Corwin's eyes grew wide. He could tell it wasn't a howl at all. It was the sound of someone screaming in pain.

He glanced nervously around the shop. "Show yourself!" he yelled. He clenched the bat in his sweaty palms and waited for a reply, but none came. Instead a racket erupted upstairs.

Boom! Meow!

"Trash! Slim!" Corwin called as he raced upstairs. He entered the living room where he found both of the cats hunkered under the bed, hissing at the desk, now lying on its side. The camera, the lamp, and the box, all lay scattered across the floor. No one else was in the room.

Corwin made a room-to-room search, turning on all lights as he did, but the house was empty. He returned to the living room and picked up the box.

The ring was gone.

He heaved the desk right-side up, then began picking up the papers, pens, and other baubles that had been scattered. Finally, he shined a penlight under the couch and removed the floor vent covers, but found no sign of the beetle.

He rose to his feet and heaved a sigh of relief. Trash and Slim peeked out from their hiding spot and eyed him suspiciously.

"Don't look at me that way, boys," he said. "It's right where it should be—lost."

1
FISH-GIRL
AND MEOWS

"'Time for a Superpowered Somer-Assault, Meows!'
Fish-Girl said. The bad guys freaked out when Meows
flipped through the window with a crash. 'Oh, no!'
they yelled. 'Those windows were supposed to be cat-
proof!' Then another window exploded as Fish-Girl
crashed through. 'Your windows may be cat-proof,
but no window is Meows-proof!' she said."

Jonas rolled his eyes. "Give me a break," he muttered. He leaned forward in his chair and stretched
his arm toward the ceiling.

"'Look out!' Meows screamed to Fish-Girl. A trap
door opened and a bunch of zombies leaped out. Fish-
Girl backed away because she was scared at first, but
then she smelled something good. 'Hey, those zombies smell like a cookout!' Meows said. 'You're right,
Meows!' Fish-Girl said. She knew the smell was hot

dogs. The smell made her super-hungry. Suddenly she wasn't scared of the zombies, she wanted to eat them because they were hot dog zombies."

"What?!" Jonas yelped. The man stopped reading and noticed Jonas's hand was raised.

"Jonas Shurmann, is there something you would like to add to this story?" the man asked.

"Mister— I mean, Edison. Cats can't somersault," Jonas declared. "It's impossible. And the glass would cut Fish-Girl and Meows. Broken glass is really sharp and dangerous."

"I see," his teacher said. "Funny that you should find Miss Hazari's story lacking in realism. I could easily say the same about your story."

"The stuff Sejal is writing is impossible," Jonas said. "I know, because I have adventures with real cats and I've almost been cut jumping through a broken window."

Jonas ignored the ripple of laughter that passed through the classroom. He was telling the truth. Jonas Shurmann was a local superhero. Less than two months ago, his father had given him a chicken costume for Halloween that somehow allowed him to talk to and understand cats. And with that costume, he became partners with two local cat detectives named CatBob and Neil Higgins. Together, the trio had been on a couple of adventures where they helped both cats and humans, the first of which had made the local newspapers.

Edison shook his head. "*The Adventures of Fish-Girl and Meows* is a work of fiction, Mr. Shurmann. Sejal tells us so right on the cover. But you, Jonas," he said as he lifted Jonas's paper from a stack on his desk, "you submitted *The Dusenbury Curse* as a work of non-fiction and I find many things in your story to be impossible." He stopped in front of Jonas's desk. "Do you see what I'm getting at?"

Jonas's nose twitched and he coughed. Edison smelled bad, but no one had been able to say what exactly he smelled like. "The difference is that I didn't make it up," Jonas said.

Edison narrowed his eyes, then laughed. "Cats don't break into people's houses and steal things the way you describe in your story. If they did, how would pet stores stay in business with all of the marauding feline thieves scampering off with their food, toys, and catnip?"

The class burst into laughter. Jonas glanced around. Even his friend Danny Martin was laughing.

"Much less all of the mice, gerbils, rats, birds, and all of the fish," Edison added. "Pet stores would be one big all-you-can-eat cat buffet!"

The class roared with laughter.

"But my story is all true," Jonas protested. "You can ask Orville Dusenbury. He was there. He saw it with his own eyes."

"Yes, and if I recall your story correctly, Orville was the only person present to witness the alleged theft." Edison perched on the corner of his desk and knit his brows. "How do you know he was telling the truth? You didn't even see it. Could it be that he was mistaken or even, well, dare I say..." He cocked his head.

"Orville would never lie!" Jonas snapped. "He's one of my best friends and he needed our help. We know Dasza stole from him because she had his deed in the Zookeeper's house."

Edison frowned sympathetically and adjusted his thick eyeglass frames. "I'm certainly not accusing Orville or anyone else of lying, Mr. Shurmann. I'm merely suggesting that you should use your vivid imagination to entertain your classmates, instead of trying to convince them that you have superpowers."

Jonas set his jaw. He was so angry he couldn't speak.

"You're a good guy, Jonas." Edison patted him on the shoulder. "We all like you, even if you aren't really a superhero. Right, class?"

The children nodded hesitantly. Danny Martin

and his friend Seth yelled, "Fish-Girl and Meows are awesome!" from the back of the class.

"Agreed!" Edison said with a wide smile. "Which is why you're all getting copies of this exciting first story to take home to critique." He waved a stack of photocopies.

A bell tone announced the end of the school day. As each group of busers and walkers were dismissed, Edison handed out copies of Sejal's story. Jonas snapped his copy from Edison's hand and jammed it into his backpack.

"Enjoy, Mr. Shurmann!" Edison sang. "See you tomorrow."

Jonas grumbled to himself and shuffled down the hall. He grabbed his coat out of his locker and heard a rip as he tugged it on. He grumbled again at the separated shoulder seam, then yanked up the zipper and pushed his way through the front doors.

A gust of frigid wind slapped his face as he stomped down the steps. He stopped when he felt something jabbing him in the shoulder. He turned to find Sejal Hazari standing behind him. "Oh, great! It's you," he said. "What do you want?"

Sejal shifted her weight. "I just want you to know that, um," she stammered. "I just wanted to say I liked your story, *The Dusenbury Curse*."

Jonas scowled. "I didn't do anything to you. Just

leave me alone!" He hoisted his backpack over his shoulder and walked away, sniffling at the cold air.

He was trudging past the idling school buses when the bark of a car horn startled him. He looked over to find his friend, Orville Dusenbury, seated behind the wheel of a sleek, black car. Orville smiled and waved through the tinted glass. The window slid down and loud music spilled out.

"Hop in, Drumsticks!" Orville shouted. "Your dad couldn't make it, so the Heavy Metal Express is here to rock your face all the way home!"

Orville was an adult who lived in an old mansion on East North Dusenbury Street. Jonas and his partners had met him on their first case together and since then, they had all become best friends.

Jonas opened the door and flopped into the passenger seat. Screeching guitars roared from the speakers. He winced and covered his ears. Orville laughed and stopped the music with a tap of a button.

"Sorry," Orville said. "Things are getting pretty cramped at Castle Dusenbury with all of my house guests, so I took some time away today. I'm getting ready for Pizza Night early."

"Oh, yeah," Jonas mumbled.

Jonas liked Orville because he wasn't like other grown-ups. He was usually happy and he liked to do fun stuff like play video games, eat pizza, and goof off. And he really liked cats. In fact, his house guests were actually a whole colony of cats that Jonas and his partners had discovered living in the ruins of an abandoned amusement park that Orville's family owned. The cats had been staying in Orville's house for about a month.

Orville's mischievous smile dropped from his face when he saw Jonas was upset. "What's up with you?" he asked with sidelong glance. "You got girl trouble? Is it that girl I saw you talking to?"

"No! Gross," Jonas said.

"Hey, that's the girl who moved in across the street from Tallula, right?"

"Yeah, Sejal Hazari. She's the super smart new kid that's so perfect," Jonas sneered.

"So what's got you so down?" Orville asked as he swung the car into the street. Jonas remained silent. "Okay, that's fine. We don't have to talk about it. Hey!" he said, sitting up in his seat, "I picked up an X-Box today for Tallula's place and a copy of *Smash-Lord III: Ninja Empire*! Now, with a little practice, she can join in on the tournaments. Isn't that awesome?"

"Sejal's making fun of me to the whole class with her stupid stories," Jonas shouted. "And Edison is making copies for everyone and saying the story I wrote is a big lie. It's not fair!"

"Wait, what?" Orville exclaimed. He could see Jonas's eyes were misty. "Slow down, CB. What's going on?"

"Sejal wrote a story about a superhero named Fish-Girl who has a supercat named Meows," Jonas said. "And even though the story is totally impossible and stupid, everyone loves her story and they think my story is a big lie because Edison said it is."

"Who's Edison?"

"He's my teacher," Jonas said. "He's the substitute for Miss Keys and he's horrible. We have to call him by his first name and his cologne smells disgusting. He said you lied about Dasza stealing from you and that I'm trying to trick my class into thinking I'm a superhero!" Jonas wiped his eyes. "He made the other kids laugh at me."

Orville knitted his brows. "If Sejal's new to your school, she's probably making her own version of the Chicken-Boy and Crime Cats to show she thinks you're cool."

Jonas shook his head.

"As for the other thing," Orville said. "Is your teacher from around here?"

"I don't think so," Jonas answered.

"Well, see, he's new too. He's not hip to the Chicken Power—yet—but he'll get there," Orville said. "Not every neighborhood has a real-life super-hero. In fact, I'm pretty sure Clintonville's the only one that I know of. And it's pretty crazy, so not everyone's going to believe it at first."

"I guess so," Jonas said. "But he still stinks."

"It'll be fine. Trust me." Orville jabbed him in the ribs with his elbow. "Plus, I got a little something for you while I was out today."

"Really? What is it?"

"Well, I was going to save it for the holiday, but it looks like you can use a little surprise today." Orville smiled. "But first, we have to do something."

"What's that?"

"We gotta go heading out to the highway!" Orville announced as he punched the power button on the stereo. The opening riff to his favorite Judas Priest anthem roared from the speakers. Jonas spent the rest of the drive playing air guitar and drums while Orville howled and screamed behind the wheel.

When the song ended, Orville dropped Jonas at his house with a blue plastic box labeled "Kinetic Sand."

2
THE
INVITATION

Orville was wrong. Things weren't better the next day. Not for Jonas, at least. But for Sejal Hazari, the new kid at Clinton Elementary, things couldn't have been better. Every kid at school was talking about Fish-Girl and Meows. Everyone wanted to know if Sejal could bring the supercat to school. And some of the younger kids Jonas had seen pretending to be CatBob and Neil Higgins during recess, now argued over who would be Meows.

Then things got even worse. Edison announced that their school would host the premiere of a new skeleton exhibit that would travel all over Ohio. Some guy who attended Clinton Elementary a long time ago had teamed up COSI, the science museum downtown, to create the exhibit. And because this was such a big deal, Edison said everyone had to write a report on archaeology or history. This wasn't so bad, because Jonas was actually interested in archaeology, even though he hated the pressure of big assignments. But then Edison added that the reports had to be written by teams.

He read off a list of each team and when he announced Sejal was Jonas's report partner, the classroom erupted into giggles. Jonas glanced back at the corner desk, where Sejal sat, blushing.

Then Edison said the worst thing of all. He explained that the team with the best report would have to give a short presentation in two weeks at the unveiling ceremony. Jonas sank in his chair. Sejal was the teacher's pet, so Jonas was sure their report would be chosen. And Jonas got really nervous when he had to talk in front of people—even his class.

Jonas broke into a sweat as he imagined Sejal forcing him onto the stage to give the presentation alone with no report. News crews would crowd in, pointing cameras and lights in his face. He would see his parents—everyone's parents—watching him in the audience, waiting for a great report, but he wouldn't have it. Instead, he would just stand there, mumbling nonsense, trying not to throw up. Then Edison and Sejal would start laughing at him and everyone else would join in. Jonas imagined looking around and seeing the dinosaur skeletons from the exhibit coming to life, pointing their little arms and wagging their gigantic jaws as they too cackled at him. He was so lost in his daydream that he hadn't noticed school had been dismissed. It wasn't until he heard Edison calling his name that he realized he was sitting alone in the classroom.

"Are you all right, Jonas?" Edison asked.

"Yeah," Jonas mumbled as he walked to the door.

"Don't forget this." Edison grabbed an envelope off of Jonas's desk and handed it to him.

"What's this?"

Edison shrugged. "It was on *your* desk."

Jonas waited until he was at his locker to examine the envelope. It was addressed to him, CatBob, and Mr. Neil Higgins. He opened the envelope and removed an invitation to dinner and a sleepover at Sejal Hazari's house Friday night.

Jonas slipped the card in his backpack and glanced around the hall. He expected to catch sight of Edison, peeking around the corner wearing a big "I gotcha" grin, but no one was watching him. He looked for Sejal but couldn't find her either. He pulled on his coat, slung his backpack over his shoulder, and made for the door.

Jonas spent the walk home lost in his thoughts once again. He was sure the invitation was a prank.

It had to be. He was afraid if he asked Sejal about it the next day at school, she would pretend not to know what he was talking about. Or, she really wouldn't know because Edison had actually written the card. But even then, she might think Jonas had made the fake card to invite himself to dinner. And then she would think he was biggest weirdo in school and would ask Edison for another report partner. Then Jonas would get a bad grade because no one else would want to be his partner either.

Jonas came to when he heard someone call his name.

"Hey, Jonas!"

He looked up and saw a woman with long, black hair smiling down at him. It was his friend, Tallula Kobayashi.

Jonas frowned. "Hey, Tallula."

"What's wrong? Are you still having girl trouble?" she asked.

"Yeah, and Orville said it would get better, but guess what? It's only gotten worse. Edison made Sejal and me partners for a big report."

Tallula smiled. "I heard this Sejal's been giving you a hard time. Take it from me, Kiddo, when a girl gives you a hard time it's usually because she likes you."

"Ugh, gross!" Jonas groaned. He fished the

invitation from his backpack. "I think she left this on my desk at the end of school."

Tallula read it and smiled. "Well, it's cool that she invited the boys to come along." She then bent down and spoke in a hushed voice. "Let me know what their house is like," she said. "I've always wondered what it looks like inside, but it sold so quickly I didn't even get to see the realtor's photos."

"I don't know if I'm going," Jonas said. "I have to see what CatBob and Neil think. I'm on my way there now. Well, see you around."

A few minutes later, Jonas was brought into the living room at Neil's family's house, where he found his feline partners lying on separate floor vents. The cats saw him and leaped to their paws. Neil meowed his greetings and gave Jonas tail-hugs while CatBob squinted and whispered little meows. Jonas spent the first few minutes sitting on the floor dealing out pets and hugs before CatBob settled in his lap. The peachy feline rumbled with delight as Jonas ran his hand from the top of the detective's pointed head to the crooked tip of his broken tail. Neil Higgins, on the other hand, was contented to lie on the floor, letting Jonas rub his golden belly. The snowy winter had forced his partners to stay inside most days, and all that time spent eating and lying on floor vents had caught up with them.

"You seem anxious," Neil said Jonas remove his knit cap and pulled up the feathered hood of his costume. "Is something the matter?"

Jonas frowned. "This new girl at school, Sejal, wrote a story about a girl with a magic fish costume named Fish-Girl."

CatBob pushed his cheeks forward in a smile. "She must be a fan," he said.

Jonas shook his head. "Fish-Girl has a sidekick— a supercat named Meows who saves other cats from having to take baths."

Neil thwacked his tail and swiveled his ears. "Save cats from baths? Preposterous!"

"Are other cats bathed so much that they need saving?" CatBob asked.

"That's just it!" Jonas said. "Her story is full of totally unrealistic stuff, like cats somersaulting through windows and hot dog zombies—and everyone loves it. But they think *The Dusenbury Curse* is fake."

"Well, they're wrong," Neil sniffed. "We all know what happened."

"Yeah, and we have witnesses," CatBob put in.

"Then today, at the end of school, I got this invitation." Jonas took out the card and opened it.

"Invitation?" Neil asked as he nosed the card. "Is Sejal the girl that wrote the story about this

Meows character?" he asked.

"Yep."

"So just don't go to whatever it is," CatBob said.

"The invitation is addressed to Jonas Shurmann *and* CatBob and Neil Higgins." Neil said.

CatBob pawed at the card. "It's to *all* of us?"

"Yes," Neil said. "It's an invitation to dinner and a sleepover."

"I guess she wants to see what real hero-cats look like!" CatBob exclaimed.

"And the invitation does specify dinner," Neil said. "Well, we certainly wouldn't want to be rude. No one likes rude heroes."

Jonas frowned. "No one at school thinks we're heroes anymore. My teacher passed out copies of Sejal's story to the whole class and now Fish-Girl and Meows are more popular than us."

Neil cocked his head. "So, why is that bad?" he asked.

Jonas hesitated. "I don't know. I guess it's not. I just..."

"We help the neighborhood cats and our human friends like Orville because we care about them," Neil said. "Not because it makes us popular. I know I don't mind not being popular."

"I know, but..." Jonas breathed.

"It's nice when people pay attention to you," Cat-Bob said.

Jonas smiled. "Yeah, it is."

"But if you spend all your time trying to make everyone like you," Neil said, "you'll have no time to make yourself happy."

* * *

That night, a strange noise broke Jonas's troubled sleep.

Blop! Blop!

His eyes shot open and scanned the room but he didn't see anything out of the ordinary. He lay still for a few minutes, waiting and listening in the dark.

Blop! Blop!

There it was again. Jonas slowly sat up and saw that the plastic box of Kinetic Sand that Orville had given him the day before was open. He crept over to his desk where he discovered the sand had been dumped all over his schoolbooks.

Blop! Blop!

Jonas watched as bubbles rose from the surface of the sand and popped, as if it were a boiling liquid.

Blop! Blop!

Jonas scratched his head. He had played with the sand the day before and it hadn't bubbled then. The grains were very fine, almost like flour, and it was almost wet to the touch, but it wasn't really wet. It was weird stuff, for sure, but it didn't bubble. Jonas switched on a lamp and watched as the sand began to ripple. Then it shrank into a smaller pool all by itself. More bubbles formed in the middle of the pool.

Blop! Blop! Blop!

The bubbles rose and burst in a rapidly rolling boil and Jonas could see an image was forming in the bubbles. A bug—a beetle—emerged then disappeared. He leaned in closer. Another image began to take shape. A human skull stretched its jaw open and Jonas heard a scream from somewhere far away. Then the image vanished and the bubbles stopped.

The sand was still.

Jonas reached down and pinched the skin of his arm. He winced. He was awake. He carefully stepped up to the desk and examined the sand that lay in a lump on his math book. He picked up a pencil and poked it. The pencil's eraser left an indentation.

"Weird," he breathed.

A hand shot from the surface of the sand and grabbed his arm. Jonas yelled and stumbled back. The fingers released him and the hand dissolved into millions of granules on the desk.

Jonas tumbled backward out of his room and into the hall.

"Jonas, are you okay?" his mom called from the bottom of the stairs.

Jonas hesitated. He was scared, but he also realized he didn't want his parents taking the sand away from him. "Um, yeah Mom," he shouted. "I just—I saw a spider." As soon as he had caught his breath, Jonas charged downstairs and swiped an empty jar from the kitchen pantry. He swept the sand into it, screwed the lid on as tight as he could then placed the jar on his desk. From his bed he watched the jar for more movement but nothing happened.

He grabbed his phone and texted Orville.

WHERE DID U GET THIS SAND?

3
THE SAND SPEAKS

Jonas tried not to walk too close to Sejal Hazari as the pair made their way down the hall. He was still angry with her for robbing him and his partners of their popularity, but anger wasn't the only emotion he was feeling. In fact, Jonas was overwhelmed by so many feelings that he wasn't sure what to do or how to act.

He just stared at the floor as they walked, silently thinking about all of the things he wanted to say to her. Yet no matter what he managed to think of or how much he wanted to say it, Jonas couldn't speak a word. Instead, he kept stealing glances at her. She was always pushing the same strand of hair behind her ear and every time she did, Jonas noticed the scars on her elbows and the long scab running down her forearm. He was about to ask her wounds when she suddenly spoke.

"Can you believe Edison is letting us see the exhibit before it opens?" she asked. "These skeletons have been in Corwin Bachert's family for like, 100 years."

"Really? How did he get them?" Jonas asked.

"His great-great-great-grandmother, Helen Aldrich, and her husband, Edgar. Edgar Aldrich was born in Clintonville and became an electrical engineer. He made a bunch of money from the trolley cars that ran from downtown Columbus to Olentagy Amusement Park." She looked over and smiled. "But you probably knew that because of your story about the Dusenbury brothers."

Jonas had never heard of Edgar Aldrich before, but he nodded anyway.

"They moved after that and Edgar ended up making a lot more money from hydroelectric power plants and fruit plantations. When he retired, he was old—like, 40—but he was a millionaire. So he took Helen and traveled around the world three times and they got all of the bones during their adventures."

"How do you know all of that stuff?" Jonas asked.

"I researched Clintonville's history as soon as my father told me where we were moving," Sejal said. "It's a very interesting place."

"Yeah," Jonas sighed. "I guess."

"Says the boy who dresses up in a chicken costume to solve mysteries."

Jonas stopped and turned to Sejal. "At least I try to help people," he said. "I don't make fun of them just to be popular."

Sejal spun around. "I've never made fun of you. I wrote Fish-Girl and Meows because I had read the newspaper stories about you and the Crime Cats and I assumed that's what everyone would be writing about."

Jonas eyed her suspiciously, unsure if she was telling the truth. Could it be that Orville was right after all?

"I didn't know Edison was going to make copies and pass them out to everyone," she added. "I didn't ask him to and I sure didn't write it to be popular." Sejal looked down at the floor and hugged her notebook. "I've never been popular at any other school."

Jonas nodded. "Me neither," he said. "Well, until I got the chicken costume. Then I was popular...for a while. But now everyone likes Fish-Girl more."

"It doesn't matter," Sejal said. "Spiderman is popular too, but he's not real. You are, and a real superhero is always cooler."

Jonas smiled. "Do you think?"

Sejal nodded. "So are you coming to my house for dinner Friday?"

Jonas looked down at the floor. "Yeah, I think so. And CatBob and Neil said they want to come too."

Sejal smiled. "Really? My father will be so happy. He's really excited to meet them. Oh!" She grabbed Jonas's arm and became very serious. "Don't forget. The cats have to take a bath before dinner. Will that be a problem?"

Jonas looked down at Sejal's hand. "I don't think so."

"Good!" She released him. "My mother will freak out if they aren't bathed. She sort of obsesses about germs. That's why we're not allowed to have any pets."

"Cats are pretty clean," Jonas said. "They bathe all the time."

Sejal shook her head. "My mother said cats aren't clean, they're just covered in cat spit."

Ms. Harless, the school librarian, greeted them at the gates. She read their pass and ushered the pair behind the plastic sheets that hid the exhibit from view.

"The workmen are on their lunch break," Ms. Harless said, "so you have ten minutes before they kick you out. If you need anything, let me know." Before she disappeared behind the plastic sheet, she touch."

Jonas looked around and frowned. He didn't see any dinosaur skeletons looming among the scaffolds and glass cases. He had assumed the collection would include dinosaur bones for some reason. He hadn't expected anything as big as a Tyrannosaurus Rex, but he had hoped for at least a Velociraptor. After the initial disappointment wore off, he followed Sejal around to inspect each case individually.

The first case held a human skeleton that stood about as tall as Jonas. The spine was held upright by a metal rod that ran down into a wooden base. A second rod held a small plaque stating the skeleton was that of an 8-year-old boy from Egypt.

"Weird!" Jonas said. "Is that what I look like inside?"

"You look exactly like that," Sejal said with a smile, "if your muscles, veins, blood, skin, and hair didn't get in the way. But they do and that's why you don't freak everyone out."

Jonas laughed.

The next case held the bones of a huge snake. Thousands of tiny ribs curled out from a spine that spiraled around the support rod a full two feet taller than Sejal and Jonas. The pair leaned in to examine the tiny skull perched atop the vertebrae. The jaw was stretched open to expose rows of long, rectangular teeth, not the snake fangs Jonas had expected.

"What kind of snake is that?" Jonas asked.

"The plaque says it's a reticulated python, which are found in Southeast Asia," Sejal said. "'Arthur'—that's this guy's name—was brought back by the Aldriches during their visit to Bali."

"Cool," Jonas whispered.

The third case was the largest. It held the skeleton of "Fancy," Helen Aldrich's favorite horse. The skeletons that followed were still in the process of being assembled by the workmen. They included frames of smaller domestic animals, like birds, bats, owls, cats, and dogs. But it was the last case that caught Sejal and Jonas's attention. Jonas pressed his face to the glass case and read the plaque.

"Awesome!" he whispered. "It's a real saber-toothed cat."

The dark brown bones were positioned in a dramatic pose as if the beast were lunging at its prey. The jaws gaped open, giving onlookers a clear view of the 9-inch yellow canine teeth.

"Wow!" Sejal whispered.

"I know," Jonas added. "I can't wait for CatBob and Neil to see this." His nose twitched. Something smelled bad. He looked around and noticed a reflection in the case move. He spun around to find Edison standing behind them, taking a sip from his coffee cup.

"Ahhh. Just got a fresh cup and thought I would see how you two are getting on. This really is something, isn't it?" he asked, leering at the cases. "It's like George Clinton Elementary has its very own museum now. The unveiling ceremony will be a really big deal. Have you two managed to decide on what aspect of archaeology your report will focus on?"

Jonas shrugged.

"Well, you had better decide soon. This report will be a big part of your overall grade for the year." He lifted a coffee cup to his lips and blew into it as he walked over to the plastic curtain. "Do hurry. The workmen are very busy and our next lesson will begin soon," he said as he slipped out of sight.

Jonas looked at Sejal with wide eyes. "Did you hear him come in?" he whispered.

Sejal shook her head. "Weird, huh. But he's right. We need to decide on our report. I think we should do it on King Tut because Edgar and Helen Aldrich were actually there when Tut's crypt was opened."

"Really?" Jonas asked.

"Yes. And Helen was the first woman to enter the crypt."

"King Tut is fine with me," Jonas said. "Mummies are cool."

"Oh! and one other question," Sejal added. "What do the cats like to eat?"

* * *

That evening, Jonas sat in his room, peering through the jar on his desk. The sand wasn't moving. He flicked the glass with his finger.

Thonk!

Nothing.

Jonas looked over his shoulder to make sure his bedroom door was open, in case he would need to escape, or at least call for help if something crazy happened again. He was comforted by the noises of his dad washing the dishes in the kitchen downstairs.

He looked at his phone. Orville had answered his text from the night before.

TOY STORE. SAND IS FROM SWEDEN. WEIRD STUFF, HUH?

It sure was. Jonas took a deep breath, carefully grabbed the jar with both hands, and lifted it. Again, the sand remained still. He set his jaw and gave the jar a few hard shakes. The sand settled instantly and remained motionless. Jonas waited a few minutes but nothing happened, so he replaced the jar on his desk and got ready for bed.

Crash!

Jonas's eyes shot open at the sound of shattering glass. He sat up in bed to find raindrops pelting his window and the thunder rumbling in the distance. Gusts of wind moaned through the eaves. Jonas scanned the room and saw that the jar of sand wasn't on the desk.

He leaped out of bed and stopped when his toes squished into the ultra-fine grains. He looked down and discovered that the shattering sound had been the jar. Shards of glass stuck out from the dunes that covered the floorboards.

Oh, great! he thought. *Dad's going to go crazy when he sees this.*

A flash of lightning revealed the sand was rippling as it had before. Jonas backed away as the grains began to swirl and churn. The surface became choppy, like a stormy sea, then it suddenly froze. Jonas kneeled down and examined the phenomenon. The grains had not formed waves, but little houses, trees, and cars all lining a street—an oval street. Jonas recognized the place. It was Nightshade Court. Everything was in perfect detail, except for a single shard of glass that stuck out of the oval median of grass that the street encircled. It gleamed in the flashes that flickered through the window.

Jonas turned to grab his phone to take a picture,

but realized he had forgotten it in his coat. When he turned back, the sand had gone flat. It was just a mess on the floor. Jonas tiptoed over to his bookshelf and grabbed a metal box.

The box was actually a small blue safe with a red combination dial on the front, like the one on his school locker. He read the combination that was scrawled in marker on the bottom and opened the door. He dumped a few crumpled dollar bills out into his desk drawer then began to scoop up the sand with sheets of paper.

The safe's door barely shut, but with some effort, Jonas finally managed to close it. Then he spun the dial and placed it on his desk. Once the broken glass was in a wastebasket he laid down and fell right back to sleep with a smile on his face.

4
PRINCESS
SASCHA

Warm temperatures the next afternoon seemed to have all of Clintonville melting. The winter world Jonas had so enjoyed turned into one big, muddy slush puddle. The treads of Jonas's shoes were caked with mud by the time he made it home. He kicked his sneakers onto the floor vent, washed an apple, and checked for new posts on the *Clintonville Social Network*.

Jonas and his partners spent most afternoons searching for cats that had been reported missing on the web site. They also got help from neighbors, thanks to the official Crime Cats profile that his dad had helped him set up.

Jonas saw a new post for a long-haired black cat named Princess Sascha who had just been reported missing an hour before. Jonas looked out the window and sighed. He wolfed down his apple and slipped on his raincoat and galoshes. A few minutes later, he was picking up CatBob and Neil, who weren't excited about leaving the dry, padded chairs on CatBob's porch.

"I know you guys don't like taking the bike," Jonas said, "but the sidewalks are huge mud puddles, so you'll have to ride in the backpack. But at least you won't be cold."

His partners reluctantly piled into the bag and the trio set off.

The search was slow. Standing water on the sidewalks forced Jonas to pedal slowly to keep the rear wheel of his bicycle from throwing water up into CatBob's and Neil's faces as they scanned the yards. Plus, daylight didn't last long during the winter and it was getting close to dinnertime for his partners. Jonas felt the contents of his backpack squirming as he turned a corner.

"Do we need to stop for a pee break or do you see something?" he called back.

"Let us out," Neil cried. "I think I see her!"

Jonas dismounted from his bike and unzipped the bag. The felines leaped out and sniffed the ground and air.

A small, clear meow chimed from a crop of bushes growing against a nearby house.

"Sascha?" Jonas called.

A pair of yellow eyes appeared among the branches.

Jonas crept closer and held out his hand. "Come out, Sascha. We're here to take you home."

A small black cat leaped out onto the walkway. Her big, fancy tail unfurled as she sniffed Jonas. She then presented herself for pets and purred when he ran his hand over her silky back.

"The name is *Princess* Sascha and I'm ready to go home. It's boring out here—and gross," she said. "I don't know why my family makes it snow and rain like this. It's like they love ruining a perfectly good day. I don't know how many times I've asked them why and they never give me an answer."

CatBob and Neil came over and sniffed at the newcomer. Upon seeing the detectives, Princess Sascha crouched low and hissed.

"It's okay," Jonas said, reassuringly. "This is CatBob and Neil Higgins. They're detectives and they're here to help get you home."

"Ugh! And another thing I don't like about being outside—cats!" she spat. "I'm not a stray, boys. Just keep walking."

"Some cats..." Neil said, shaking his head.

"Well, you'll all have to share my backpack on the ride home," Jonas responded.

Sascha's ears swiveled on her head. "It's bad enough getting my paws wet out here. I'm not returning home smelling like stray cats too."

"They aren't strays," Jonas said.

"Don't waste your time, Jonas," CatBob whispered.

"It's not that far to your house," Jonas told Sascha. "You're just going to have to put up with it." He reached down to pick her up but she hissed and swiped at his hand. Jonas jerked his hand back. "Hey! Don't scratch me. I'm trying to help you."

"You're not stuffing me in your hobo cat bag," she snapped. "Find another way and hurry up; it's getting dark out."

Jonas reached out again and Sascha responded with a growl and a raised paw.

"Take it easy," Jonas said. "I won't pick you up. I'm going to call your family to come and get you."

"Fine!" She thwacked her tail on the ground while Jonas flipped her tags around and read them.

He took out his phone and dialed the number. A few seconds later he was assuring the woman on the other end that Princess Sascha had been found safe. When she asked where she should meet them, Jonas realized they were on Nightshade Court. After the call ended, he looked around and found the street was exactly as the Kinetic Sand had showed it the night before.

He told his partners to stay with Sascha and crossed to the large oval median. The snowmelt had left most of it submerged under a muddy pool now dotted by small islands of frozen snow. Jonas sloshed out to the middle and looked around. He spied a larger lump of ice peeking out of the water and kicked it with his boot.

When the mud settled Jonas saw something smooth break the surface. He kneeled down and chipped away chunks of ice until it was free. He cupped the treasure in his hands all the way back to his partners.

"Hey! Check it out!" he called as he reached the driveway. "I found a ring, I think." He kneeled down and presented a small stone beetle that sat perched on a copper band. CatBob and Neil nosed it for a moment, then backed away.

Sascha hissed. "Don't dig up what someone else buried in the litter box," she said.

"Jonas, how did you know to look for that?" Neil asked.

"I—I didn't," Jonas stammered.

CatBob eyed him suspiciously.

Just then, a white car pulled up to the curb. The door swung open and a woman hopped out. "My little princess—they found you!" she squealed.

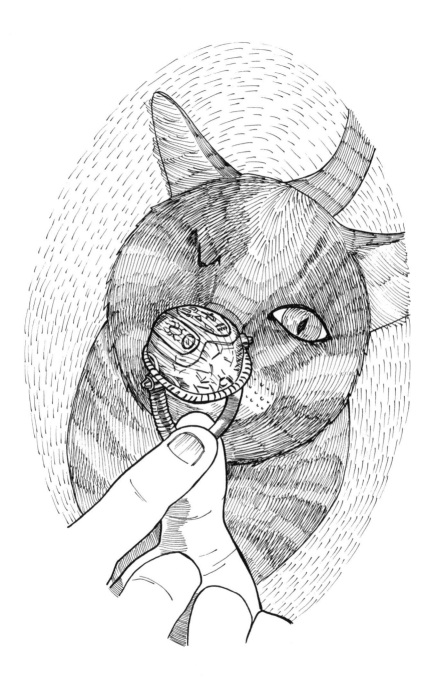

Sascha trotted merrily over to the woman and leaped into her waiting arms.

The woman turned to Jonas. "Thank you so much for finding my little princess," she said. "I thought I was going to die. You really are a superhero." She crouched down and smiled at CatBob and Neil. "Thank you, too, Crime Cats!" she sang.

She then shook Sascha in Jonas's face and spoke in a high-pitched voice, pantomiming Sascha speaking. "Thank you for finding me, Chicken-Boy," she squeaked. "I'm going to tell everyone what a super—"

Sascha hissed and swung at Jonas, leaving a pink line across his cheek.

"Sascha!" the woman cried. "I'm so sorry. Are you okay?" she asked Jonas.

Sascha growled, promising more violence to come.

Jonas touched his cheek but felt no blood. "I think so."

"She gets cranky when she's hungry," the woman said. "But you probably know all about that, right?" she nodded to Jonas's partners, who sat patiently at her feet.

Sascha cackled. "Just because it's buried, doesn't mean it's treasure. Just ask your stray friends."

The woman placed Sascha in the cat carrier that

sat in the passenger seat of the car and thanked Jonas and his partners before speeding off around the median and out of sight.

Once they were gone, Jonas looked down at his partners and frowned. "What was with her?"

"Some cats are solitary creatures," Neil said. "They just do not like the presence of other cats."

"Princess Sascha definitely needs to stay indoors," CatBob added. "And that's where we need to be, too. It's Feastable Time!"

Jonas loaded his partners into his backpack and headed home. By the time he parked his bike in the garage, it was past his dinnertime. He strode in through the back door and was promptly stopped by his dad.

"Whoa! Take your boots off, Chief," Mr. Shurmann said, pointing to the muddy trail Jonas had left on the floor. "That's not going to be fun to clean up."

"Sorry," Jonas panted. "The boys and I found a missing cat," Jonas said. "I just dropped them off at their houses."

"Then I'll bet you're hungry," Mrs. Shurmann called from the dinner table. "Put your boots on the porch and go get washed up."

Jonas slipped off his boots and did as he was told. After he cleaned the mud off the floor he told his parents about the rescue of Princess Sascha over a delicious taco dinner. All except the part about finding the ring and the Kinetic Sand. He had meant to tell them—he just forgot. By the time he remembered, he was in bed, drifting off to sleep.

* * *

The next day at school, Jonas was summoned to the principal's office. He sat slumped in a chair, trying to think of why, but he couldn't remember doing anything wrong.

A beep sounded from the principal's assistant's desk. She answered her phone, mumbled into the receiver, then nodded and hung up.

"You can go on in, Jonas," she said.

Jonas opened the door and found Principal Wells at his desk with Edison standing beside him. Both men looked concerned.

As soon as Jonas took his seat, Principal Wells asked him what he and Sajel had done the day before during their visit to the bone exhibit. Jonas recounted their visit just as it had happened, including Edison's mysterious appearance. When he finished, Principal Wells asked him if he was absolutely certain that was all that happened. Jonas nodded.

"At this point, we're just interested in getting

back the bones," Principal Wells said.

"Getting them back?" Jonas echoed, confused. "What do you mean?"

"The workmen arrived from lunch to discover two of the exhibits had been vandalized," Edison said.

"Yes." Principal Wells shook his head. "Bones were stolen. Jonas, I would like you to take Edison to your locker and bring your book bag back here."

"But I didn't take anything," Jonas said. "I told you—"

Principal Wells raised his hand and nodded toward the door. Jonas rose and shuffled out of the office and down the hall with Edison following close behind. Jonas pulled his backpack from his locker and the pair returned to the office a few minutes later. Edison unzipped the book bag and dumped its contents onto Principal Wells's desk.

The two men frowned. The desk was covered by a heap of books, notebook pages, pencils, erasers, and a couple of tattered comic books.

"No skull," Principal Wells muttered.

Jonas's brows rose. "Skull?" he asked.

"The skull from the human skeleton is missing as is the entire body of the reticulated python," Principal Wells said. "I'm sorry, Jonas, but you and Sejal were the last two people seen in the exhibit before the workmen returned." He looked up at Edison, who shook his head. He then began replacing the contents of Jonas's bag. "You're sure you didn't see anyone in the halls?" he asked Jonas. "Any strangers?"

"I didn't see anyone," Jonas replied. "And Sejal was with me the entire time, so I know she couldn't have taken anything. Plus, what would you put that huge snake skeleton in without being noticed?"

"I don't know," Principal Wells said as he handed the backpack to Jonas. "I guess we'll let the police figure that out."

Jonas wanted to tell both of the men that something weird was going on. He wanted to tell them about the skull, the map, and the hand that formed in the Kinetic Sand. He even had the urge to tell them about the ring, but he knew they wouldn't believe him—especially not Edison. He would laugh it off and insist it was all Jonas's overactive imagination. So Jonas said nothing. He just took his bag and sauntered out the door.

On the way back to his classroom, a strange sound caught Jonas's attention. He stopped and cocked his head to listen. Just under the muffled voices that crept from behind the classroom doors, he could hear something that sounded like a stick in the spokes of a spinning bicycle wheel. But it echoed as if it were far away. He looked around the hall but didn't see anyone or anything that could be making the noise. When it stopped, he continued on, but heard it again as he turned toward his classroom. This time it sounded as if the noise was coming from the air vent in the ceiling.

"Hello?" he called up to the vent.

There was no reply. The noise grew faint and finally stopped.

5
THE
HAZARIS

"Meows!" Neil yowled. "Help me, Meows!" The portly feline squirmed in Mr. Shurmann's hands as he was lifted from his carrier. "I'm sorry I doubted you, Meows! Help!" The detective growled as he was swung over the edge of the sink. "Meows, save me!"

"Shush!" CatBob hissed from the next sink. "I thought you said Meows was ridiculous."

"I called him preposterous," Neil corrected. "And he is. But if he saves me from this bath, I'll take back everything I said. This is worse than being put in the Pinchy Cage!"

"You're overreacting," the peachy feline said.

"No, I'm not, Bob!" Neil howled as his butt touched the water. He kicked his feet, splashing water everywhere. Mr. Shurmann plopped the gray feline down and he instantly became silent.

"See," CatBob said with a smile, "I told you. The water feels great."

"Oh, shush!" Neil shot back.

After their baths, the felines were dried and given claw trimmings before being placed back in their carriers. From Jonas's mom's veterinary hospital, Mr. Shurmann drove the trio down to High Street, across from Phoenix Books, Tallula Kobayashi's home and business.

According to Tallula, the rambling, white brick house Sejal's family had moved into had previously been an art gallery. And it was still a gallery, according to the new sign in the yard that read NORTH OAK GALLERY: FINE JEWELRY AND RARE ANTIQUITIES, DR. NIRAV HAZARI, PHD.

Jonas turned to his dad. "What does 'PhD' mean?" he asked.

"It means Sejal's dad is a really smart guy," Mr. Shurmann replied. Then his father leaned over and whispered. "Tallula's family are Indian, right?"

Jonas eyed his dad. "Yeah, why?"

Mr. Shurmann motioned to the glow from the fast food restaurant that lay just beyond the overgrown bushes at the edge of the cramped yard. "Hindus consider cows sacred. They don't eat meat. I can't imagine a Hindu family would live next door to a

44

burger place."

Jonas knitted his brows.

"If they are, don't tell them I'm going next door after I drop you off," Mr. Shurmann whispered. "It smells way too good to pass up. I'm starved!"

Jonas rolled his eyes and pressed the doorbell. Deep chimes rang and faded away.

The clacking of several deadbolts was followed by the appearance of a bald man in an argyle sweater vest, who peered at Jonas and his dad through outdated eyeglass frames.

"Welcome, Shurmanns!" he exclaimed. "Please, come inside. We don't want our guests of honor freezing to death, do we?" He ushered them through an enclosed porch and into a foyer, where Sejal appeared and took Jonas's bedroll and overnight bag while he got out of his hat and coat.

Mr. Shurmann introduced himself to Mr. Hazari and his wife, Rushma, who looked like a tall version of Sejal. Finally, Jonas introduced his dad to Sejal before Mr. Shurmann made his exit.

Once the handshakes and farewells were over, Jonas kneeled by the cat carriers and addressed his hosts.

"This is the first time we've been invited anywhere, so I don't know if CatBob and Neil are going to feel weird being in a new place. They may stay in their carriers for a while. Just don't take it personally. It's how cats are."

"Wait!" Rushma cried. "I'm sorry," she said, kneeling next to Jonas, "but I need to know if they have been bathed."

"Rushma, please," Dr. Hazari said. "They're fine. It's not every day that our daughter's heroes come to dinner."

"Dad—Shhh!" Sejal slapped her dad on the arm.

Jonas looked up at Sejal, who was hiding her face in her hands. "I, uh—" he stammered. "We just bathed them and trimmed their claws at my mom's veterinary hospital."

"Thank you," Rushma said. She heaved a sigh of relief and then motioned to Jonas. "Go ahead. Let's meet these famous cats."

As soon as the door was opened, CatBob sprang out. He looked around and sniffed the air and the carpet.

"This is CatBob," Jonas said. "CatBob, meet the Hazari family."

The peachy feline meowed his greetings.

"May I?" Dr. Hazari asked Jonas as he bent down to pet CatBob.

"You'll have to ask him," Jonas replied. "Just let him sniff your hand first."

CatBob sniffed, then headbutted Dr. Hazari's

hand. A huge smile crossed the man's lips.

"Sejal, come feel his coat," he whispered excitedly. "It's so soft!"

"And the final member of our trio is Mr. Neil Higgins," Jonas announced as he swung the other carrier door open.

Neil waddled out, looking everyone over and sniffing at the air.

"What happened to his eye?" Rushma asked.

"That's not polite dinner conversation, my dear," Dr. Hazari said. "Besides, I think it makes him look more dashing. Gives him character." He reached out to Neil, who gave him a few sniffs and then walked over for pets.

"It's just a cat," Rushma said.

"Not just any cat, Mom," Sejal said. "The Crime Cats have solved two mysteries so far."

"Nonsense, girl," Rushma shot back. "Don't humor your father's fantasies."

Dr. Hazari gave Jonas a rueful smile. "That is the burden every hero must bear. There will always be people who will doubt you." He looked over at Rushma, standing with her arms crossed, and shook his head. "You cannot allow them to shake you. They will recognize you in time."

Jonas nodded and then looked down at Neil. The cyclopean feline wore a knowing smile.

"If there are no hairballs to clean up in the morning, I will be happy!" Rushma announced. She then excused herself and headed back to the kitchen while Dr. Hazari invited his guests to tour the gallery.

He first took them into a room where a series of glass cases stood under inset lights. The cases contained all sorts of jewelry. Most of it was made of gold and silver that sparkled under the lights, but other pieces were too old to sparkle. They didn't look pretty, just old and brown—sort of like the beetle ring.

Dr. Hazari also showed off some old paintings from Europe by guys Jonas had never heard of and a small collection of jewelry and figurines from ancient Egypt. In particular, Dr. Hazari pointed to a large necklace with metal plate that had a beetle engraved into it. He explained it was his most prized piece.

"And we'll get to figure out how old it is and use the data for our report on Egypt," Sejal said.

"Oh, cool!" Jonas said as he leaned forward to study the engraving. The beetle looked different than his ring. Maybe the ring wasn't from Ancient Egypt.

A short time later, the trio was brought to the dining room, where Rushma had a huge feast prepared. The table was set for all of the guests, including CatBob and Neil Higgins.

"The animals each have a piece of cooked fish and a chopped shrimp and scallop," Rushma said. "They are plain. I read on the Internet that oils and spices are bad for cats, so no curry for them."

"Wow, guys! Your own cooked meal," Jonas said as he lifted them onto the table. "What do you think of that?"

The cats meowed and chirped as they sniffed the air and then their meals.

Jonas turned to Rushma and smiled. "They thank you very much. They said the food smells delicious."

"Tell them they are welcome as long as they don't step in any of our food," she replied.

"Maybe they should have worn shoes," Dr. Hazari said. "Rushma's cooking is spicy enough to burn the bottoms of your feet!" He laughed and invited Jonas to help himself.

This was Jonas's first time eating Indian food so he relied on Sejal to guide him through the dishes. And despite her warnings, he insisted on trying some of everything. This resulted in Jonas occasionally gulping glasses of milk to extinguish his tongue when the stronger spices set his mouth ablaze. But once he had worked through the burn and the ensuing sweat, Jonas enjoyed the meal.

Jonas's face lit up with surprise when he tasted a spoonful of spicy meat.

"Oh, my gosh! You're not vegetarian, are you?" Sejal said. "I forgot to ask."

"No," Jonas said as he swallowed. "I was just surprised. My dad told me—"

"Oh, we're not vegetarians," Dr. Hazari chimed in. "We are Hindu, but not all Hindus are vegetarian."

"If we were, we would never buy a house next to a hamburger restaurant," Rushma added.

"Which is why grandma about had a heart attack when she saw this place on Google Maps." Sejal said.

Rushma narrowed her eyes at Dr. Hazari, who smiled in return.

"It smells delicious and ensures visits from my in-laws are short," he declared. Then he asked Jonas how he became a superhero.

Jonas told the story of how he got his chicken costume and how he had met his partners, who had by that time finished their meals and were content to fill in bits of the tale while they groomed on the floor.

Jonas then explained the history of Olentangy Park and the Dusenbury brothers, who were ancestors of his friend Orville. "The park stood where they're building those new apartments and the grocery store," he explained.

Dr. Hazari was so fascinated by Jonas's story that he couldn't stop asking questions. When it was obvious Jonas was getting overwhelmed, Sejal stepped in. Her father apologized and explained that his interest in Jonas and the cats stemmed from his study of the Ancient Egyptians.

"It was forbidden to kill a cat in Egypt," he explained as he chewed. "The Greek historian Herodotus wrote that he once witnessed a Roman soldier make that very mistake. The soldier was soon surrounded by an angry mob bent on avenging the feline's death. The Pharaoh himself pleaded to the citizens to spare the Roman's life, but it did no good. He was torn to pieces in the street."

Dr. Hazari looked over at Neil and smiled. The stoic feline sat, silently watching him. "They are so handsome," he said with a big smile. "Do you know why the Egyptians valued cats so highly?"

Jonas shook his head and translated the question to his partners.

"Protection," CatBob meowed.

When Jonas translated for Dr. Hazari the man practically leaped from his chair. "Yes!" he said. "Exactly."

Neil meowed at Dr. Hazari and all eyes went to Jonas.

"He says the only reason CatBob knew that is because Neil told him."

Dr. Hazari shook his head in wonder. "There would have been no Egyptian Empire without cats," he continued. "Cats guarded early villages against poisonous snakes and rodents. It was thanks to that protection that their civilization survived and flourished."

"Wow," Jonas whispered.

"And when a cat died," Dr. Hazari added, "their family mourned just as they did when a human family member passed away. They sometimes shaved their eyebrows off to express the sadness of their loss. And the cat was given a burial just like a human: they were mummified."

"Dad," Sejal said, "tell them about the temple of Bast!"

"Yes, yes," Dr. Hazari continued, "I'm getting to it. So, a great temple was built for Bast, the Egyptian cat god, along the River Nile. And in 1888, a huge crypt under the ruins of that temple was discovered by a farmer. 80,000 feline mummies were discovered inside."

"80,000?" Jonas exclaimed. "So there's a museum somewhere with 80,000 cat mummies?"

Dr. Hazari furrowed his brow. "No. A few went to the Natural History Museum in London but the rest were..." he rubbed his hands together, "ground up! Made into fertilizer, unfortunately."

Jonas frowned. "Well, I guess it would be hard to get people to look at 80,000 cat mummies in a museum. There probably aren't 80,000 human mummies."

"More!" Dr. Hazari exclaimed. "Almost one million human mummies have been discovered, and about as many cat mummies. What does that tell you?" He waved his spoon playfully in the air, pointing to CatBob and Neil. "The Ancient Egyptians loved their cats, because without them, their empire would never have lasted 30 centuries."

"Wow, Dr. Hazari, you know tons about Egypt," Jonas said. "So, if someone had something really old, you could look at it and tell them if it was from Ancient Egypt, right?"

"Of course. It's my job." Dr. Hazari nodded.

"Do you think you could look at something for me?"

6
IT LIKES YOU

After the meal, Rushma set to work clearing the table while Dr. Hazari led Jonas and Sejal to his office, with CatBob and Neil trailing behind.

Dr. Hazari flipped on the lights and motioned to the white examination table in the center of the room. He lifted the cats onto the table then clasped his hands together. "So, Jonas, let's see what you've got."

Jonas produced the beetle ring and laid it on the table. Dr. Hazari raised his brows and swung his magnifying lamp around. He switched the light on and peered into the glass.

He turned the ring this way and that under the lamp, occasionally giving a "hmmmmm" or a "huh," before straightening up to address Jonas again. "This certainly is an interesting piece," he said. "May I ask where you acquired it?"

"It's not mine," Jonas said. "It actually belongs to a friend of mine. He's kind of rich. He was curious and I'm kind of doing him a favor. I hope you're not mad."

"Don't be silly." Dr. Hazari waved his hand. "Not at all."

"So, is it Egyptian?" Jonas asked.

"At first glance, it would appear so," Dr. Hazari said. He positioned the lamp lower and invited his guests to take a look.

Jonas, Sejal, CatBob, and Neil all crowded around the lamp.

The ring looked enormous through the magnifying glass. The lens seemed to expose every tiny detail, no matter how small. Jonas spotted tiny nicks and cracks in the surface of the stone that he hadn't noticed before. And Dr. Hazari's fingers were so big that Jonas could count each of the grooves that made up his fingerprints.

"Do you see these hieroglyphs carved into the shell?" Dr. Hazari asked.

Jonas had noticed there were a number of tiny symbols etched into the beetle's back. One was a bird and one looked like a feather, but he hadn't been able to identify them clearly.

"This is the cartouche of Tutankhamun," Dr.

Hazari explained. "It is how the ancient Egyptians wrote his name. It is pronounced, KHEPERU-NEB-RA."

"Does that mean this was King Tut's ring?" Jonas asked.

Dr. Hazari laughed. "I doubt that," he said as he handed the ring back to Jonas. He rose and grabbed a book from a shelf. "All of the treasure from Tutankhamun's crypt was photographed and cataloged by Howard Carter, the archaeologist who conducted the expedition. And you can see here," he said as he spread the book on the table, "there is no such ring in this book."

Jonas frowned through the glass. He turned the ring over then slid it onto his finger. The wings snapped open with a click.

"How did you do that?" Neil asked.

Jonas shrugged. "I don't know. They just opened up."

Dr. Hazari took Jonas's hand in his own and examined the ring again. "It likes you," he said. "This is extraordinary. I don't think I've ever seen anything like it. Ancient or not, your friend certainly has a fascinating piece here. Would you mind if I kept it for a couple of days? I could probably find out where it came from."

"I don't know," Jonas said. He retracted his hand

and slipped the ring off. "My friend was weird about me taking it out of his house in the first place."

"That's understandable," Dr. Hazari said, as he ran his hand down CatBob's spine. The peachy feline pushed his cheeks forward into a smile and rumbled with satisfaction.

Jonas looked at Sejal and then placed the ring back on the table. "You can borrow it, Dr. Hazari."

"Are you sure?"

Jonas nodded.

"Thank you. I'll do my best to find out what I can. And until then, you can give my card to your friend." Dr. Hazari slipped a business card from his shirt pocket and handed it to Jonas. "I can't promise anything, of course, but I'll tell you what I find—"

Dr. Hazari was cut short by a shrill screech. Jonas started and looked down to see Neil pounce on CatBob and bite him.

"Hey!" Jonas yelled. "Break it up."

A second later Neil was on the opposite side of the table, staring out the window as if nothing had happened while CatBob licked his shoulder.

"What was that?!" Rushma called from down the hall.

"Nothing," Sejal replied. "The cats were playing."

"I fed them sufficiently," Rushma yelled. "It will

not be my fault if they eat each other. And you and your friend will have to clean it up, Sejal."

"Mom!" Sejal cried as she rolled her eyes.

Jonas stroked CatBob's back. "Are you okay, Bob?" he asked.

"Yeah, I'm fine," the peachy feline replied. "Neil just gets frisky sometimes."

Jonas crossed the table, where Neil sat gazing out the window. He rubbed the detective's round head. Neil craned his head up to direct Jonas's fingers to his nose. "Are you okay, Buddy?" Jonas asked.

"Please tell the Hazaris I'm sorry," Neil said. "I don't know what came over me. I'm sorry if I startled everyone."

"I think we'll survive," Jonas said. "But remember, we're guests tonight. You'll have to pick another night to eat each other."

Neil nodded to CatBob, who had crept up and was rubbing against him. "It'll be tough," the cyclopean feline said. "CatBob did taste delicious."

After that, Dr. Hazari announced that he was kicking everyone out so he could get to work on the ring. He told Sejal to take Jonas upstairs to fetch her sleeping bag and choose a movie to watch.

Jonas and his partners followed Sejal upstairs to the end of the hall where they stopped at a door covered with a poster of a man on a skateboard flying in mid-air. A wooden plaque rested atop the door-frame with Egyptian hieroglyphs painted on it.

Jonas pointed to the plaque. "What's that say?"

"Death shall come on swift wings to him who disturbs the peace of the King," Sejal said a spooky voice. "That was what was carved over the entrance to King Tut's tomb. It's the curse of the Pharaoh."

"Why do you have it above your door?" Jonas asked.

"To keep my mom out," Sejal said. "Too bad the curse isn't real. Most people that entered Tut's tomb died of old age and I'm pretty sure it hasn't kept my mom out of here even one day."

Jonas heaved a secret sigh of relief. If the beetle ring did belong to King Tut, Jonas was glad to learn there was no curse attached to it.

"Of course, Lord Carnarvon and the Aldriches did die shortly after they entered the crypt," Sejal said as she opened her door. "So maybe there is something to it."

Jonas tried to laugh, but a lump had suddenly formed in his throat. He swallowed hard. "Weird," he croaked. He turned and pointed to the poster on the door. "So, who's that guy?"

"That's Tony Hawk," Sejal said. "He's the greatest skateboarder in history."

She flipped on the light and invited Jonas in. "This is my room," she said.

Sejal's bedroom was mostly what Jonas had expected a smart girl's room to look like. There was a desk with a computer on it, two big bookshelves crammed with books, and a pink bed crowded with stuffed animals. But he hadn't expected the three skateboards leaning against the wall. He walked over to the desk where two sets of skateboard wheels lay next to some small tools. He picked up one of the wheels.

"I'm working on my boards so they'll be ready for a trip to the indoor park," Sejal said.

"I didn't know you skateboard," Jonas whispered.

"You can't tell?" She turned her arms to show the scars on her elbows and the scab running down her forearm. "My mom hates it because she says I always look like I've just been in a car accident." She rolled her eyes. "Do you skate?"

Jonas frowned. "I've never really tried," he said. "I have a BMX, but I can't really do any tricks." He glanced around the room. "Do you play video games?"

Sejal shook her head. "No, my mom won't let me because she thinks they're too violent. Plus, my father says they'll only distract me from schoolwork."

"My parents don't allow me to have them either," Jonas said. "But my friend Orville loves video games, so I play over at his house all the time. Lately we've been playing *SmashLord III: Ninja Empire* and I'm undefeated."

"Really?"

"Yeah, it's this awesome fight game where you get crazier moves the more enemies you defeat. We always have tournaments, but I always win because I invented a move no one can beat. Orville calls it the Felonious Flip-Kick Whammy Buster."

Sejal laughed.

Jonas walked to the window and took out his phone and began punching buttons. A few seconds later, his phone chimed.

"Turn off the light," he said.

Sejal flipped the switch and Jonas pulled the curtains aside. He brought Sejal over and pointed to the house directly across High Street, where she spotted two people waving from an upstairs window.

"Those are my friends, Orville and Tallula," he said. "Tallula lives there and Phoenix Books is her store."

Sejal waved back to them.

"Do you want to go over?" Jonas asked.

"My parents will never let me," she said. "It's too late."

"But what if we had to? Like an emergency."

"What do you mean?"

"Well..." Jonas said, looking down at CatBob and Neil, who were circling around his legs, "I think your mom forgot one thing for the sleepover."

"Litter boxes!" Sejal whispered.

"Yep. And unless she wants a mess—"

"No!" Sejal yelled. She caught herself and paused. "Sorry. Don't even think about it. She would freak out. I would be grounded for life."

"Well, I happen to know a place with two litter boxes just across the street."

7
OPERATION: LITTER BOX

A little while later, Jonas and Sejal were in front of the TV, watching *Indiana Jones and the Raiders of the Lost Ark*. They jumped when Dr. Hazari snuck up behind them and shouted, "Cover your heart!"

"That's from *Temple of Doom*, Dad!" Sejal said.

"I know," Dr. Hazari replied. "I just needed to distract you while I get a snack." He jammed his mitt into the bowl of popcorn and hoisted a fistful away into the darkness.

"Dad!" Sejal cried.

"Shhhh! You'll wake your mother," the voice called from behind them, "and nobody wants that." Dr. Hazari's footfalls faded down the hall and ended with the sound of his office door clicking shut.

Jonas turned to Sejal and whispered, "Operation: Litter Box is a go!"

They pulled on their coats and boots and slipped out the back door with CatBob and Neil eagerly leading the way.

"We have to hurry," CatBob said. "I've held off Pee-Pee Cat Time as long as I can."

"Thanks for holding it, Buddy," Jonas whispered.

They were greeted at High Street by a hooded figure in a dark robe. Jonas hoisted Neil while Sejal carried CatBob across the street and up the steps to the front door of Phoenix Books. The Hooded Figure pushed open the door and beckoned them to follow.

CatBob and Neil cried and squirmed as soon as they were inside and disappeared as soon as they were released.

"My mom forgot to get litter boxes," Sejal said. "Thanks for letting us bring CatBob and Neil over. I think my mom would die if they went on the floor."

"No problem," the Hooded Figure replied. "I can take your coat."

"Okay," Sejal said as she unzipped, "but we can't stay long. If my dad finds out we left, he'll freak."

"I think he'll be busy for a while," Jonas put in.

"Come on up." The Figure folded their coats in its arms and led them up a staircase.

The sweet smell of chocolate filled the stairwell

as they reached the second floor. A door swung open and the warm glow of firelight came spilling out. As soon as they entered the room, Jonas and Sejal's attention was drawn to a frosted Christmas tree that crowded the corner. Its blinking branches sheltered stacks of presents wrapped in shiny, foil paper.

Orville Dusenbury leaned forward in a high-backed leather chair, pounding a video game controller with his thumbs. His gaze was locked on a huge TV screen above the fireplace mantel that showed Orville's ninja warrior punishing his opponent with a flurry of kicks and punches. Within a few seconds, Orville's adversary lay unmoving on the ground. Orville rose to his feet with his arms outstretched in victory.

"Oh, yeah! The Dusenbury Dive-Bomb takes him out!" he shouted. He turned to face his guests and smiled. "Hey, Drumsticks! Decided to share your sleepover fun with us?"

Jonas nodded. He introduced Sejal to Orville and Tallula, who returned with the hood of her robe pulled back.

"Cool robe," Sejal said.

"Thanks!" Tallula said. "Do you guys have time for some cookies?"

"Sure," Jonas said, "but I might not be able to taste them."

Sejal smiled. "Jonas had his first Indian meal tonight and my mom's cooking is pretty spicy."

"If you think it hurts now," Orville laughed, "wait until it comes back out."

Tallula rolled her eyes and laughed. "Have a seat you two," she said, "I'll be right back."

"So, have you played *SmashLord III* before?" Orville asked.

Sejal shook her head.

"Her parents don't allow her to play video games," Jonas explained.

"I'm allowed to play them...I think," Sejal corrected him. "I'm just not allowed to have a game system at home because they're afraid it will distract me from my school work."

"It totally will," Orville said. "But you can have some fun tonight. *SmashLord III: Ninja Empire* is way better than *SmashLord I* or *II*." He handed the controller to Sejal. "Jonas can show you the basics. He's the best player here."

Orville stood up and turned around as CatBob and Neil Higgins slipped into the room. "I thought I heard my main beasts!" he said. The cats cried as they scampered over and went to work rubbing against his corduroy pant legs and giving him tail hugs.

A few minutes later Tallula returned with a

platter full of warm cookies and tall glasses of cold milk and the party got underway. And it turned out, Sejal wasn't bad once she got the hang of the basic commands. Everyone took turns playing each other but no one came close to beating Jonas. Every match he played ended with his warrior using his bo staff to launch himself into the air while Jonas yelled, "Bock-bock, chicken!" Then his warrior would spin like a horizontal tornado, delivering super-fast kicks to his opponent. No matter what maneuver was taken to counter it, Jonas's guy would knock his opponent out every time.

Sejal smiled. "So that must be—"

"The Felonious Flip-Kick Whammy Buster!" Orville and Tallula answered in unison.

"No one has figured out a way to stop it," Orville said. "But when I do, Fight-O McDuffins will be history!"

"Who's Fight-O McDuffins?"

"That's Jonas's character's name," Orville explained. "See, once you find the fighter you play the best with, you have to come up with a good warrior name. The name is part of the way you get better. My guy was named Victor von Shinsplints, but that name didn't make him a better fighter. But now that his name is Baron von Broheim of Buttkickistan, he wins a lot more matches."

"Don't feel bad," Tallula said, "I haven't thought up a name yet either, but I'm new to the game, too."

Sejal was munching one of the last cookies with Neil curled up on her lap when she looked at her phone and saw three hours had passed. "We have to get back before my dad leaves his office again!" she shouted.

Everyone sprang to their feet and hurried down the stairs. The kids were put into their coats and shepherded back across High Street by Tallula. As they slipped through the back door, and they heard noises coming from Dr. Hazari's office.

"Hurry!" Sejal hissed as she dragged Jonas toward the living room.

The pair managed to dive into their sleeping bags and tear off their caps when the office door opened and Dr. Hazari came creeping down the hall. They heard him pause at the living room before continuing up the stairs to the second floor.

"That was close!" Sejal whispered.

"Yeah, it was," Jonas said. "I thought we were busted for sure."

CatBob and Neil came over and pawed at Sejal's and Jonas's faces.

Jonas laughed. "What's up, guys?"

"We're cold," Neil said. "Let us in your bag."

"I don't think there's room for both of you."

"I have room," Sejal whispered. She unzipped her bag and opened it. CatBob crawled in, turned a few times, then curled up next to her. She laughed. "He's so soft, his fur tickles," she said.

"I know," Jonas whispered. "Neil is purring so loud I can feel it in my belly."

"Good night, Neil," Sejal whispered.

A muffled meow came from Jonas's bag and sent both of them giggling.

"Good night, CatBob," Jonas called.

The peachy feline called back.

Then silence fell and all that could be heard was the muffled sound of passing cars and the occasional whoosh of air from the floor vents. Then a gurgling sound came from Jonas's sleeping bag. He shifted. "Oh, great," he whispered.

"What's wrong?" Sejal asked.

"Now *I* have to use the litter box."

8
FLIGHT
OF THE
SCARAB

Dr. Hazari awoke in a fit of coughing. He held his smart phone to his bleary eyes to read the time: 3:00 AM. He rolled out of bed and hurried downstairs, doing his best to muffle his wheezing barks with his pajama sleeve. Stealing through the living room on tiptoe, he cut between Sejal and Jonas as they lay fast asleep in front of the TV.

Once in the kitchen, he dove for the sink, and gulped water straight from the faucet like a dog until the tickling in his throat stopped. Satisfied, he rested his weight against the counter, heaving deep breaths and wiping the water from his chin. Outside, a strange noise rose. It sounded as though the wind was howling through the eaves of the house, but when Dr. Hazari peeked out the window, he found the trees standing motionless against the night sky.

He poured a glass of water from a pitcher and took a long drink as he walked back into the living room.

He leaned over Sejal's sleeping bag and gave her a peck on the cheek.

The howling noise outside grew louder and was joined by a distinctly different noise—one inside the house.

The sound was coming from the end of the hallway, where Dr. Hazari's office was. He crept down the passage and discovered the office door standing ajar. He narrowed his eyes. Dr. Hazari always kept his office door shut.

He slowly pushed it open and leaned in.

A shaft of moonlight spilled through the window, and landed on a tall, thin figure that stood hunched over the examination table. It swayed from side to side, as if dancing to an unheard rhythm.

Dr. Hazari reached for the light switch, but no illumination accompanied the click. The noise only alerted the intruder to his presence. The figure whirled around and Dr. Hazari saw two hollow sockets staring back at him.

A grinning skull clutched Jonas's ring in its teeth.

Dr. Hazari shivered. He opened his mouth to scream, but all that came out was a small croak.

Then a brilliant blue flame burst from the skull's

eye sockets, nose and mouth, sending the doctor stumbling back. As he did, the figure pushed past him and slithered down the hallway.

"Hey, stop!" Dr. Hazari cried as he raced after it. But when he reached the living room, he found no sign of the intruder. Sejal and Jonas remained asleep on the floor. He bent down and shook Sejal.

"Sejal, wake up!" he hissed. "There is an intruder in the house." But his daughter's eyes remained closed and her breathing remained steady.

Dr. Hazari looked around and caught the tail of the figure's shroud slipping out of sight at the top the stairs.

He charged up the steps and rounded the corner just in time to spot a shadow disappear into Sejal's room. He stopped at a hall closet door and drew out a golf club, then quietly removed his flip-flops.

He held the sand wedge at the ready as he crept down the hall, straining his eras to hear anything beyond his own thundering pulse. The house was completely silent. He couldn't even hear the air blowing through the floor vents anymore.

Dr. Hazari leaped into the room with the club held high, but no one was there. Jonas's overnight bag lay open on the floor. Articles of clothes had been scattered on the bed. Dr. Hazari carefully scanned the room and noticed that the pile of stuffed animals

Sejal kept on her bed had been disturbed. He stepped toward the bed and examined each one.

Bunny rabbit...kitty cat...Teddy bear...unicorn...human skull!

The figure sprang from the bed, sending the plush dolls raining down on Dr. Hazari. He swung his club wildly, missing everything but the lamp on Sejal's desk. Shards of glass went flying across the room.

Dr. Hazari chased the figure back through the hall and down the stairs. "Rushma," he yelled as he ran, "call the police! Kids, stay back!"

Back in the living room, he found Sejal and Jonas still asleep on the floor. He leaped over the couch and bolted into the kitchen, where he cornered the figure against the counter.

"Give me the ring!" he huffed. "Hand it over now!"

The skull's mouth opened and a dry, husky voice spoke. "Save the ring or save them," it croaked. "You must choose...now."

Suddenly, Dr. Hazari heard a scream come from upstairs.

"Rushma!" he yelled.

Then he heard Jonas scream in the next room, followed by Sejal.

Dr. Hazari hesitated, then turned and ran into the

living room.

He shook Jonas and Sejal. "I'm here, children. Wake up!" he cried.

Sejal's eyes shot open and she threw her arms around her father's neck.

Jonas awoke a moment later, drenched with sweat and gasping for air.

Dr. Hazari picked them both up and made his way upstairs where he awoke Rushma.

"What's gong on?" his wife asked.

"There was an intruder," Dr. Hazari huffed.

"An intruder?! We have to call the police." She leaped from the bed and ran down the hall with Dr. Hazari chasing after her.

"No! You musn't go down there," he called, but it was too late. He found Rushma clutching the phone and staring at the back door, which was swinging wide open.

Dr. Hazari heaved a sigh of relief. "Good. It's gone," he breathed.

"*It?*" Rushma asked.

* * *

Dr. Hazari waved good-bye to the policemen, then shut the door and staggered into the kitchen. He poured a fresh cup of coffee and yawned.

"So what did they say?" Rushma asked.

"It's weird—very weird," Dr. Hazari replied. "The detective said he found no footprints in the snow in the back yard, but the back door—there," he said as he nodded to the door just behind Rushma, "is obviously how the thief got in and out."

"Why was the back door open?" Rushma asked as she turned to Sejal, who sat quietly eating a bowl of cereal.

"I, uh...I probably forgot to close it last night," Dr. Hazari replied.

"What were you doing in the back yard?" Rushma eyed her husband suspiciously.

He shook his head and rolled his eyes. "I might have snuck out for a cigarette...and must have forgotten to lock the door."

"Nirav! You said you had quit."

"I know," he said. "I was working late and excited about the ring..."

"What about the ring?" Sejal asked.

Dr. Hazari's hand trembled as he wiped his mouth. "I don't know. I'll call the insurance company Monday. Until then—"

His words were cut short by his wife. "Until then, Sejal, you are forbidden to speak to Jonas Shurman."

"Mom—that's not fair!" Sejal cried.

"I don't care if it's fair or not," Rushma said as she rose and dumped her mug in the sink. "The very first night that boy is in our home, he brings filthy cats, the house gets robbed, and I have nightmares of skeletons shooting blue fire."

Dr. Hazari stared at his wife.

She looked at him with narrowed eyes. "What?"

"No—Nothing," he stammered.

"Mom—" Sejal began to protest, but heeded her father's gesture to stop.

Rushma shot her daughter a warning look and left the room.

Sejal pushed her bowl away and began to cry.

Dr. Hazari frowned. "She's only doing what she thinks is best for you."

"It's not fair," Sejal said. "I finally made a friend and we had fun and now Mom wants to ruin it."

Dr. Hazari leaned close and spoke in a hushed tone. "Yes, so much fun you two forgot to lock the back door after you snuck back in last night."

Sejal's eyes grew wide.

"Your mother doesn't need to know," he said as he wiped the tears from his daughter's eyes. "She means well, but she might be mistaken in this case."

"What do you mean?" Sejal sniffed.

"You like Jonas?"

"Yes," she answered. "I think he's nice."

Dr. Hazari nodded. "I do too. But I think he's in serious trouble and he's going to need help." He leaned back and peered into the living room to make sure Rushma wasn't listening in. "I'll work on your mother, but until she changes her mind, don't let Jonas out of your sight. But respect your mother's wishes and...try not to speak to him, okay?"

Sejal smiled and nodded.

PRICELESS

That morning, Jonas awoke tangled in his sheets, but didn't bother wrestling himself free. He just lay there, staring up at the ceiling, thinking about how much fun he had with Sejal the night before and how he would probably never talk to her again.

A fuzzy paw tapped his cheek. He wiped his eyes and looked over to find CatBob sitting on the bed beside him, purring.

"Good morning, Jonas," CatBob said. "What's wrong?"

"I'm pretty sure Sejal's mom hates me," Jonas sniffed.

"Why do you say that?"

"She was really mad about the burglary and she kept looking at me all mean when she was talking to Sejal's dad. She's probably going to tell Sejal she can't be my friend."

CatBob placed his paws on Jonas's chest and began kneading Jonas's feathers. "Don't be so sure. I think Sejal and her dad really like you."

"Do you really think so?" Jonas asked as he wiped his nose.

"Sure. And I like the Hazaris," the peachy feline purred. "Mrs. Hazari's dinner was excellent!"

"Indeed it was!" Jonas turned to find Neil looming over him. "But you still haven't told us exactly what happened last night."

"I'm not really sure," Jonas huffed. "I remember dreaming about a skull with blue fire shooting out of its eyes. It was saying things, then it started laughing, and the laugh was super-scary and then I remember waking up out of breath."

"How strange! That's the same dream that woke me up," the cyclopean feline said. "And what happened next?"

"Dr. Hazari was all freaked out. He was sweating and he had a golf club. He said the house had been robbed." Jonas rolled out of bed and grabbed his overnight bag. "He said the ring had been stolen."

"The ring you found?"

"Yeah. He said he would report it to the police, but..."

"But what?"

Jonas's eyes were wide as he drew his hand from the bag. The ancient beetle ring sat in his palm. "But it's right here," he whispered.

"How did it get in there?" Neil asked. "I thought Dr. Hazari said it was stolen."

"He told me he saw someone take it from his office and he chased them around the house before they ran out the back door." Jonas held it to the light to be sure. It was his ring, all right.

"Why didn't you tell Dr. Hazari how you found it?" Neil asked.

"Yeah," CatBob put in, "or that it's yours and not your 'rich friend's?'"

"Because—" Jonas paused again and looked at the ring as he rolled it in his fingers. "I can't tell."

Jonas made his way down to the kitchen, where he found his mom and dad talking in whispers. They stopped when they noticed him come in.

"Do you want some pancakes?" his dad asked.

Jonas slumped into a chair at the table and nodded.

"And do you want to tell us what happened last night?" his mom asked.

Tears sprang from Jonas's eyes. "Sejal and I snuck CatBob and Neil over to Tallula's so they could use the litter box," he said.

Mrs. Shurmann shook her head. "Without telling Sejal's parents?"

"They wouldn't have let us leave, even though Mrs. Hazari forgot to get a litter box at the store," Jonas explained. "And CatBob and Neil had to go really bad and Mrs. Hazari would have—"

Mrs. Shurmann shook her head and rolled her eyes. "I can imagine." She looked over at her husband, who was listening from the stove. "And you just went to Talllula's so the boys could use the litter box, that's it?"

Jonas looked down at the table. "No," he said. "We ate cookies and played *SmashLord* with Orville and Tallula."

"You didn't go out alone, did you?" Mr. Shurmann asked.

"No, Tallula took us across High Street."

"So what was stolen?" Mr. Shurmann asked.

Jonas shrugged. "Something in Mr. Hazari's gallery, I guess."

CatBob and Neil looked up from their bowls and eyed Jonas. He didn't look at them.

"Well, I'm just glad you four are okay," Mr. Shurmann said. "And I think it's cute you have a little girlfriend."

Jonas wiped his eyes. "Sejal's not my girlfriend. She's my friend." He frowned. "Or at least she was."

"What's that mean?" Mr. Shurmann asked.

"I don't think Sejal's mom likes me," Jonas said, swinging his legs back and forth. "I think she thinks the burglary is all my fault. She probably won't let Sejal be my friend any more."

Jonas's parents exchanged looks.

Mr. Shurmann offered a less-than-reassuring smile. "I'm sure it will be fine," he said.

* * *

The Shurmanns didn't allow the burglary or the dreary skies to ruin their Saturday plans. After breakfast, they washed up, piled into Mr. Shurmann's car, and dropped CatBob and Neil off with their families. Then they headed downtown to COSI.

For years, Jonas could never remember what COSI stood for, so every time they went, it became tradition that he asked his mom. By now, Jonas could recite the answer along with her.

"COSI is an acronym. That means each letter of COSI stands for a word," they spoke in unison. "COSI stands for Center Of Science and Industry."

From the parking lot, Jonas could see giant signs hanging from the side of the building that depicted an ancient Egyptian sarcophagus. Huge letters touted THE TREASURE OF KING TUT.

As they trudged up the stairs, Jonas told his parents about what Dr. Hazari had taught him about mummies—especially cat mummies. When they got inside, Jonas asked the man in the ticket booth if the exhibit featured any cat mummies, but the man just shrugged.

Jonas was about to burst with excitement by the time they reached the main exhibition hall. He stared in awe at the two tall statues of Anubis, the jackal-headed god, that flanked the entrance to the exhibit.

"Wow!" he breathed. "These are huge."

"Yep, because those are just props," his dad whispered with a smile. "Come on. Let's go see the real loot."

Jonas spent the next hour silently taking in each exhibit. He was so quiet that his mom kept asking if he was okay.

Jonas was fine. He was just lost in his own thoughts, trying to figure out what King Tut was like as a person. The museum had all of the treasures the boy-king was buried with, and the plaques at each exhibit provided tons of information about how the stuff was made, but nothing about what Tut himself was like. Jonas knew that Tut was only eighteen years old when he died.

He would have only been old enough to drive a car for

two years if he lived today, Jonas thought.

It was then that they came to the artifact Jonas was most fascinated by: King Tut's death mask. The mask had been placed on Tut's mummy when he was buried. It was carved from wood and plated in real gold and depicted the king wearing a gold—and blue—striped head cloth that draped down past his shoulders. Two heads curved upward from the head-band just above his brow: one of a vulture and the other a cobra. And according to the mask, Tut wore a very long, braided beard on his chin. The funerary mask was featured on most of the posters and banners promoting the exhibit.

"Is that really what he looked like?" Jonas asked a curator, who was standing nearby.

The woman smiled and nodded. "He didn't always wear the *nemes*—that's what his headdress is called—and beard, but, yes, that's what he looked like. The mask was placed on the pharaoh so his body would be recognized after death."

"Did he wear makeup on his eyes like that?"

"He did," the woman answered. "The makeup protected his eyes from the glare of the desert sun, just like the eye black football players wear."

Jonas stared at the sculpture. Tut's features looked soft and round. The face didn't look like it belonged to a mean person.

"I bet he was a good guy," Jonas said. He reached into his pocket and felt the ring.

The curator smiled. "I bet he was too," she said.

After a few moments of reflection, Jonas turned to the woman and spoke again. "Did you know that a man and a woman from Clintonville were the first two Americans to enter King Tut's crypt? They were there when it was opened. Their name was Aldrich."

The woman smiled down at Jonas. "Actually, I did know that. In fact, we have a skeleton exhibit that will tour Ohio schools that's been donated by Edgar Aldrich's family."

"Yeah, it's at my school right now!" Jonas said. "I go to Clinton Elementary in Clintonville."

"That was the school Edgar Aldrich went to," the curator said. "You guys will be the first to see it."

Jonas nodded and then squinted up at the woman. "So how much is this stuff worth?" he asked.

The curator laughed.

"Like something small—like a ring," Jonas added. "How much would one of King Tut's rings be worth?"

Mr. Shurmann furrowed his brows. "Are you thinking of opening a pawn shop, Bud?"

The curator laughed. "You can't put a price on any of it," she said. "Because of the historical importance of these items—because they belonged to King Tut—they are priceless."

Jonas gripped the ring in his fist. "Priceless," he muttered to himself.

When they had finished with the Tut exhibit, Jonas dragged his parents to the planetarium. That was Jonas's favorite thing to do at COSI. He loved quietly pretending he was an astronaut—Major Shurmann of the Earth Federation Expeditionary Force—and that the projection on the planetarium's domed ceiling was his view from his spaceship's cockpit.

After the planetarium, Jonas insisted on ducking into the gift shop, where he found the book Dr. Hazari had shown him of King Tut's treasure. It was written by Howard Carter, the man who led the expedition to find the tomb.

"Look at that, Bud," his dad said as he thumbed through the book. "You might be able to use this for your report, huh?"

Jonas nodded.

"But, oh, look—bad news! There are only a few rings," Mr. Shurmann announced. "Not enough to open a pawn shop." He held out the book for Jonas to see.

It was true. There were only a few rings found in the crypt and none of them looked like Jonas's ring.

"You'll just have to make do opening a

sarcophagus wash." Mr. Shurmann laughed.

Jonas blinked.

"You know, like a car wash," his dad explained, "except you wash sarcophagi instead—Oh, forget it."

Jonas rolled his eyes and shook his head.

By the time the Shurmanns got their food and sat down to eat, Jonas was lost in his thoughts once again. He was both relieved and disappointed to learn that the ring wasn't from King Tut's crypt.

On the one hand, he had been excited to own a ring that had belonged to King Tut. He felt like it gave him a personal connection to the boy-king. But on the other hand, he was relieved to know the Curse of the Pharaohs wasn't attached to it. But he still wanted to know where the ring had come from. Dr. Hazari seemed to think it was something special and Jonas did too. He was sure of it. He could feel it in his fingers every time he touched it.

10
KING TUT'S
FART

That night Jonas dreamed he was stranded in the middle of a vast desert, alone. The sun's rays scorched the massive sand dunes that surrounded him and stretched off into a sizzling horizon. As he stumbled aimlessly, Jonas heard someone calling his name.

He stopped to listen, but couldn't determine where it was coming from. And no matter where he looked, he couldn't see another soul. Jonas shouted back, but the voice never changed. It just kept calling his name again and again.

The exact same dream visited him Sunday night as well. And the tossing and turning it caused left him tired and cranky by the time he shuffled through the doors of George Clinton Elementary Monday morning.

The lids of his eyes became heavy as soon as he

took his seat. The world around him seemed to move in slow-motion and he struggled to pay attention to anything Edison was saying. Then just before lunch, Jonas heard the voice again, calling his name.

"Jo-nassss."

He sat up and looked around. Edison was standing at the chalkboard talking to the class and Jonas figured he must have dozed off again. He rubbed his eyes and picked up his pencil.

"Jo-nassss."

There it was again. It was the same voice from his dream, but he wasn't dreaming now, was he?

"Jo-nasssssssss."

Jonas glanced around the room to see if anyone else was hearing the voice, but everyone else was focused on Edison—even Sejal.

He looked up. The voice sounded like it was coming from the air vent directly above his desk. A moment later, the voice stopped and another noise took its place. A strange rattling sound echoed from somewhere far away.

"Mr. Shurmann!" Edison's voice startled Jonas. "Is everything all right? You seem distracted."

"I'm fine," Jonas stammered. "I was just thinking about my report."

"Think about it at lunch," Edison said as he peered through his big, black eyeglass frames. "I need you to concentrate on me right now. Okay?"

Jonas nodded.

Jonas was surprised when Sejal sat down next to him at lunch.

"Hey!" he said. "I was sure your mom was going tell you we couldn't be friends anymore."

Sejal took a small notepad and pen from her jacket and scribbled something on a page. She held it up. It read, "She did."

The message knocked the wind out of Jonas. "So why are you talking to me?"

More scribbles. The message read, "I'm not. Get it?"

Jonas nodded. "Hey! My parents took me to the King Tut exhibit Saturday and I got a book with all of King Tut's treasure in it. We should get to work on our report. Maybe your dad can help us."

Sejal shook her head as she wrote, "My mom. Remember?"

"Oh, yeah. Well, we can work over at Tallula's. She won't mind."

Sejal nodded.

"I'll text her and let you know, okay?"

Sejal nodded.

Jonas furrowed his brows. "But how are we going to work on a report if you can't talk?"

Sejal never got to answer. Before she could lift her pen, Edison appeared.

"How is the report coming along?" he asked. "What's this new idea of yours, Jonas?"

Jonas glanced at Sejal and winced. Edison's stinky cologne was especially strong today.

"Jonas was just telling me that he went to COSI this weekend to research the King Tut exhibit," Sejal said.

Edison smiled at Jonas. "Is that right? Working on the weekend now? Well, then. I'll be expecting an excellent report." He stood up and strode away.

Sejal scribbled in her pad then pushed it over to Jonas.

The page showed a cartoon of Edison that actually looked like him. He was bent over a table talking. Stink lines had been drawn over his butt. The speech balloon above his head read, "You can study me. I smell like King Tut's fart."

Jonas and Sejal laughed so hard they fell off the bench.

After lunch, Sejal went outside for recess, but Jonas stayed behind. He wandered out of the cafeteria and down a deserted hallway. "Missing" fliers were taped to the walls for Arthur, the Python skeleton. Jonas rolled his eyes when he thought about

Principal Wells and Edison suspecting him of stealing it.

"Give me a break," he muttered to himself.

"Jo-nassss."

I was the voice again. It sounded closer now.

"Jo-nassss."

He walked farther down the hall, listening carefully, trying to pinpoint the source. At one point, he noticed Sejal standing by an exit that lead to the playground. She was talking, but he couldn't hear what she was saying. He turned away and strained his ears for the mysterious voice.

"Jo-nassssssss."

He followed the hall until it ended at a door. The sign above read JANITOR'S CLOSET. Jonas reached for the door handle and paused.

"Jonas Shurmann!"

Jonas started. He spun around to find Edison looming over him.

"What are you up to?" his teacher hissed.

"I was...um..." Jonas mumbled.

"Sejal said you were wandering the halls in a daze and here I find you attempting to get into the Janitor's Closet." Edison tutted. "Now you'll be joining me after school for detention."

11
AFTER-SCHOOL BLUES

It was no secret that Jonas didn't get the best grades in school, but he had never been given after-school detention before.

He stared across the room at Edison, who sat leaning back in his chair, feet up on the desk, wearing a smug smile on his face. He looked so satisfied with himself, it made Jonas sick.

Look at him, Jonas thought. *He's actually happy—happy—that I got in trouble.*

Jonas gnashed his teeth, biting back the urge to spit on the floor. Instead, he sat and brooded at his desk, thinking about how much he hated being stuck in detention, looking at Edison's big, dumb, stinking, smiling face.

Then something occurred to him. Edison hadn't caught him alone. Sejal had helped. *She told on me,*

Jonas thought. *What was she doing following me around? Has she been spying on me?* Jonas suddenly felt hurt. *If Sejal told on me, she's not really my friend after all. Maybe she's been working with Edison this entire time.*

Jonas thought about all that had happened lately. Sejal wrote the Fish-Girl stories and Edison had made copies and sent them home with the whole class. And because of that, Jonas and his partners were no longer popular. It all added up, but the question was, how did Jonas not see it sooner?

He balled his fingers into fists. *They're both jealous,* he thought. *They wish they were superheroes who were written about in newspapers, and not just a smelly teacher and a— a—*

Jonas sniffed and wiped tears from his eyes.

* * *

"You're late today," Neil said as Jonas entered the living room. "We were beginning to worry."

Jonas usually met his partners at CatBob's family's house every day after school and Jonas had learned any change from his arrival at exactly 3:40 PM would upset his partners, but Jonas wasn't in the mood for it today.

"Sejal tattled to my teacher and I got detention," Jonas grumbled. "But the good news is, I managed to discover some things about the ring this weekend." He dropped his book bag on the floor and flopped into a chair.

CatBob and Neil sat at his feet.

"First, the ring isn't from King Tut's crypt," Jonas began. "I found that out when my parents took me to COSI Saturday. All of Tut's treasure was cataloged by Howard Carter in a book. He was the archaeologist that dug it all up."

"So where did it come from?" Neil asked.

"I don't know yet!" Jonas snapped. "Give me some time. I'm doing the best I can. Geez!"

"I'm just curious," Neil said.

CatBob stood up. "The only person that could find out is Dr. Hazari."

"Bob's right," Neil added. "You should take it over—"

Jonas cut him off. "No way! I'm not giving the ring to Sejal's dad or anyone else. It's mine!"

The cats studied Jonas, but did not speak.

Then CatBob rose and stretched. "We're only trying to help," he said.

"Yeah, well...it sounds to me like you guys don't think I'm smart enough to figure this out," Jonas spat. "I already have enough problems with Sejal and Edison ganging up on me at school. If you two are going to join them, maybe it's time I start solving mysteries on my own."

With that, Jonas snatched up his backpack and made for the door.

CatBob and Neil followed behind to the edge of the porch.

"That's not what we meant, Jonas!" CatBob called.

Jonas turned and wiped his eyes. "I didn't do anything. I don't understand why you guys are against me too."

Jonas turned and stomped off down the sidewalk, grumbling to himself as he marched along. He stopped when he bumped into someone. "Get out of my way!" he growled without looking up.

"Jonas—it's me."

Jonas looked up to find Sejal standing in front of him.

"Oh, look who can suddenly talk," he sneered. "I see you didn't have any trouble speaking to your best friend, Edison, when you told on me."

"I asked him for help," she said. "You don't remember, do you? I tried talking to you but you were—"

"I don't need your help, Sejal," Jonas said. "No one likes a tattle-tale. Why don't you leave me alone and go back to writing your stupid little stories. I have *real* superhero stuff to do."

Jonas pushed past her and continued down the sidewalk. Sejal didn't try to stop him.

She sat down on a stone retaining wall and tried to calm herself. Something furry brushed against her arm. She looked down and found CatBob and Neil Higgins bumping their heads against her legs and hugging her arms with their tails.

"Hey, guys," she huffed. "I'm worried about Jonas. He's acting weird today. I wanted to ask him what's going on but he's being a jerk. Well, I think he is, anyway." She stroked their backs as she spoke. "But you two have known him longer than I have, so maybe this is normal for him."

Neil looked up to her and chirped, but Sejal couldn't understand him. She just rubbed his velvety nose and frowned.

"I think something's wrong, too," she whispered to the cyclopean feline.

12
THE DAY APPROACHES

That night, after dinner, Jonas spent a full thirty minutes sitting at his desk, staring at a blank sheet of paper. No matter how hard he tried, he couldn't think of anything to write. He was unable to recall most of the details from the COSI exhibit, and he hadn't had the chance to read any books about the discovery of King Tut's tomb. But the worst thing was that he didn't know where to begin.

It's hopeless, he thought. *Without Sejal to help me, there's no way I can write this report. It's impossible!*

Sadness overtook him. He missed his friend, but he just couldn't trust her anymore, not as a friend and not as a report partner. He was stuck writing the archaeology report alone, which he knew would likely result in a failing grade. Not because Jonas was a bad student—he just wasn't good enough to deliver the kind of report Edison was expecting. And the *F* he would get would cause him to flunk second grade.

This was all part of Edison and Sejal's plan. He knew it in his gut. He felt it in his bones. The thought made the spit in his mouth taste like poison.

Sejal and Edison are going to win, he thought. I'll be left back in the second grade.

He put his pencil down and reached into his pocket. He took the ring out and rolled it in his fingers.

"I'll bet Sejal and Edison didn't count on you," Jonas whispered. "You know stuff—you have to. Tell me something about King Tut." He slipped the ring on his finger and picked up his pencil.

As soon as the graphite tip touched the paper, Jonas began to write. And as he wrote, vivid pictures appeared in his mind.

He saw a party of men in white linen clothes sifting through rocks in the scorching desert sun. He watched one of the Egyptian workers run over to a man in a pith helmet, who cradled a yellow canary in his hands. Jonas could see the man with the bird was Howard Carter, the archaeologist.

The worker had uncovered stone steps leading down into a narrow passage. Jonas heard Carter announce to the workers that his golden canary had led them to the tomb. The workers cheered.

The scene changed to a village of tents under a starlit sky. In one of the tents Howard Carter's canary hopped around in its cage, flapping its wings and tweeting frantically. On the floor below, a king cobra was wrapping its slender body around the stand that held the bird's cage.

The next vision revealed the bird's tiny body lying stiff at the bottom of the cage. Carter's assistant lifted the bird with tears in his eyes. "The curse of the Pharaoh," he whispered through trembling lips.

The hairs on the back of Jonas's neck stood on end. He sifted through the pages he had written, then stacked them in a neat pile and sharpened his pencil.

He rubbed the ring with his thumb and forefinger.

"That was awesome!" he whispered. "Show me more."

Then just as before, images came flooding back as soon as Jonas began to write. This time he saw Howard Carter at the dig site, greeting a tall, thin, grayhaired man—Lord Carnarvon, the man who financed the excavation. Carnarvon was introducing Carter and his daughter, Evelyn, to his friends, a man and woman he introduced as Edgar and Helen Aldrich. He announced that they would be photographing and reporting on the discovery of the crypt for *National Geographic* magazine until the magazine's reporter arrived from New York.

Jonas then saw Edgar photographing the entrance to the tomb. Jonas recognized the hieroglyphics carved into the stone just above the entrance. "Death shall come on swift wings to him who disturbs the peace of the King," they read.

The next vision showed Carter standing in an empty chamber in the crypt. He drove a steel rod through a stone wall, then lit a candle and put it through the hole.

"Can you see anything?" Lord Carnarvon called down from the top of the stairs.

"Yes, wonderful things," Carter called back.

Then cracks began to spread from the hole Carter had made. The archaeologist backed away as fissures fanned out like spider legs and the stone began to crumble. A sinister crackle echoed through the chamber and then the wall burst into tiny pieces. Carter was blinded by the thick plume of dust that filled the crypt and billowed up the stairwell. At the surface, Lord Carnarvon, the Aldriches, and the rest of the workers recoiled as the cloud emerged in the sunlight in the form of a grinning skull.

Everyone covered their mouths and ran for cover as the cloud overtook them. For a few moments the brown haze obscured Jonas's vision. When the sunlight reemerged, Jonas saw Lord Carnarvon lying on the ground, dead. His face and neck were horribly swollen on one side. Carter and the workmen gathered around to examine the body, but a shrill scream drew their attention to a scene even more gruesome.

Something was lying among some large, jagged stones. The workers that had discovered the two strange objects fell to their knees and wailed. Jonas concentrated, but he couldn't tell what he was looking at. He spied a pith helmet lying near what looked like two bundles of bloody clothes. But then he recognized something familiar. A human hand was sticking out of one of the bundles—and it was wearing his ring. Jonas gasped. He was looking at the bodies of Edgar and Helen Aldrich.

Jonas dropped his pencil and pushed his chair from the desk. He rubbed his arms, trying to ward off the dread chill that sent him shivering. Then a sense of pride crept over him as he saw the stack of papers he had written. His mouth twisted into a smile and he caressed the beetle's smooth back with his fingers.

Looks like Edison and Sejal's plan failed, he thought. *I can't wait to see Edison's big stupid face when I turn in this report.*

It was then that Jonas realized he wasn't

actually thinking those things, he was just agreeing with them. The words were being spoken by someone else: a voice coming from...everywhere.

Don't let your guard down, the voice whispered. *Sejal and Edison will try again.*

"How do you know?" Jonas asked the voice.

They will try to get you in as much trouble as possible. Then your parents will take away your costume and Sejal will take it for herself. That's what she wants.

"Then why didn't she tattle to her parents the other night?" Jonas asked.

She was trying to gain your trust by pretending to be your friend, but it's an act. You can't trust her.

Jonas glanced around, but couldn't see anyone else in the room. Yet the voice sounded like it was coming from someone standing right next to him. He reached out to see if it was an invisible person, but his arms passed through air.

The only friend you need is me, the voice said. *Together, there's nothing that can stop us!*

"Who are you?" Jonas asked. "And where are you?"

Just then, something directed his attention to the small, blue safe sitting on his bookshelf. The one he had locked the Kinetic Sand in. He looked down at the ring, grabbed the safe, and set it on his desk.

See for yourself, Jonas. There is nothing to fear.

"I don't want to," Jonas whimpered, even as he twisted the dial and opened the door. He turned the safe over and dumped the sand out on the desk.

The sand immediately began churning, then gathered into one undulating lump. Fingers rose from the surface and then a whole hand shot out. The grainy fingers closed around Jonas's ring and tugged. The ring slipped off and disappeared into the sand.

Jonas screamed. He lifted the safe and swung it down onto the pile, scattering the grains everywhere.

"What is going up there?!" his dad called from downstairs.

Jonas dropped the safe onto the floor. "Nothing," he called back. He dashed into the hall, wrestled the vacuum cleaner from the closet, and wheeled it into his room. He unraveled the cord in frenzy, then the vacuum roared to life. Jonas felt relief when the first strip of clean floor emerged in the vacuum's wake. But after only a few passes, the motor made a grinding noise and died. A wisp of smoke rose from the machine and a faint smell of burning electronics filled the room.

Jonas heard footsteps coming up the stairs.

"What in the world are you doing?" Mr. Shurmann boomed.

Jonas turned around to face his parents, who stood

in the doorway gawking at the mess he had made.

"What's that smell?" his mom asked. "Did you just kill the vacuum?"

Mr. Shurmann looked down at the mess on the floor. "Is that the Kinetic Sand Orville got you?"

Jonas nodded.

"Why are you sweeping it up?" his mom asked.

Jonas wanted to tell them about the hand, but for some reason he couldn't. He just stared ahead as tears welled in his eyes.

"First detention and now this?" Mr. Shurmann said.

Jonas's eyes grew wide.

"Yeah, we got a call from your teacher this afternoon," his mom said. "What's gotten into you?"

Jonas felt paralyzed. He wanted to tell them about the ring, about the voice—about everything—but he couldn't get his body to respond to his commands.

His mom looked around the room. The sand wasn't just on the floorboards, it was on every toy and every piece of Jonas's dirty clothes that cluttered the floor. "I'm going to get you a broom and a dustpan and you're going to clean this up right now," she said.

"And until you can get your act together, you can forget seeing Orville, Sejal, or doing any hero stuff," his dad added. "You're grounded—effective immediately."

"But that's not fair," Jonas said.

"And it's not fair that I have to buy a new vacuum cleaner," Mr. Shurmann shot back, "but guess what I'm paying for tomorrow?"

Jonas was exhausted by the time he crawled into bed. The sand was in the trash, his toys were all put away, and his dirty clothes were in the hamper. Everything had its place, except for Jonas. He felt like he had no place anywhere.

Everyone seemed to be on his case all of a sudden. His parents were angry with him for getting detention and blowing up the vacuum, Edison was out to get him in trouble, CatBob and Neil were ganging up on him, Sejal's parents hated him, and Sejal was probably working with Edison. Jonas felt scared and alone.

It's not fair, he thought as he lay in bed, examining the ring by the moonlight. No one understands.

I do. The voice whispered from a shadowy corner in the room. *And I'm the only one you need. You saw it. We are invincible.*

"Yeah." Jonas nodded and slipped the ring onto his finger.

Sleep well, the voice said. *Tomorrow we will show them all.*

13
THE
ALDRICHES

Dinner at the Hazari residence was tense. Sejal hadn't spoken to her mother since Sunday morning when Rushma had forbidden her from speaking to Jonas.

And even though Sejal's father was understanding, and said to stick close to Jonas despite his wife's wishes, things had still turned out badly. The more Sejal tried to help Jonas, the more of a jerk he became.

Sejal felt alone. She had no one else to talk to at school. And even when a group of kids did invite her to sit with them, she couldn't do it. She didn't want new friends; she wanted Jonas back.

So after dinner, Sejal spent the evening by herself doing what she always did when things bothered her: schoolwork. Schoolwork always kept her mind off of her problems, but her escape was soon interrupted by knock at her bedroom door.

"How is your report coming along?" her father asked.

"Oh, hey, Dad. Okay, I guess."

Dr. Hazari bent down and wrapped his arms around Sejal and squeezed. He looked at the old photograph on Sejal's computer screen. It showed a white man wearing a pith helmet standing among a group of dark-skinned men clad in little more than face paint.

"Who are these guys?" Dr. Hazari asked.

"The man in the helmet is Edgar Aldrich," Sejal said. "And these guys are a tribe in Java that the Aldriches visited. I found some photos on a genealogy web site that were posted by a man related to Helen Aldrich. I'm trying to see if I can find out where he lives."

"Why?" Dr. Hazari asked.

"Because Edgar was originally from Clintonville and he and Helen were present when Howard Carter and his men opened Tutankhamun's crypt. So if—"

"So if," Dr. Hazari interrupted, "that ring is from Ancient Egypt, it likely came from him."

"Exactly," Sejal said.

Dr. Hazari smiled and kissed the top of her head. "My brilliant daughter! Come down to my office when you're done and let me know what you've found."

An hour later, Dr. Hazari answered a soft knock at his door. He ushered Sejal inside and asked if her mother had seen her.

"No," Sejal whispered, "she's watching TV."

"Good," he said. "So what did you find?"

Sejal handed him a printout. "One of the only living decedents of the Aldriches lives here in Clintonville. Corwin Bachert runs an antique shop about four blocks south of here."

"Well, then," Dr. Hazari said with a smile, "let's go shopping."

A CLOSED sign greeted Sejal and her father when they arrived at Corwin's shop.

Dr. Hazari shrugged. "I guess we'll have to come back in the morning."

"Or we can knock," Sejal said as she gave the door a hard whack and pushed a buzzer.

The clacking of turning deadbolts followed muffled yelling and pounding footsteps. A safety chain slid from its rails, then the door swung open. An older man in a thick cardigan sweater peered out at them through rounded glasses.

"Sorry, kid, but the shop is by appointment only," he said.

"Are you Corwin Bachert?" Sejal asked.

"Yes," the man answered.

"Mr. Bachert, we need to speak to you about your relatives, Edgar and Helen Aldrich."

The man shook his head. "I'm sorry. I'm in the middle of dinner."

"We're very sorry for the intrusion," Dr. Hazari cut in. "My daughter is doing a report on them for school. We'll come back later. We're very sorry to have bothered you."

He began to lead Sejal toward the car when she shook loose and jammed her foot in the closing door. "Mr. Bachert," she shouted, "something really weird is happening to my friend and I think your family may have something to do with it!"

Corwin paused and looked down at Sejal with wide eyes. "I see," he said as he opened the door. "Well, then, why don't you come in?"

After Corwin stored his dinner in the refrigerator, he joined the Hazaris in his living room, where his fat, black and white cat was already making friends.

"That's Slim," he nodded at the handsome feline that eyed him from Sejal's lap. "Trash is my other kitty. He's probably hiding under the bed." Corwin took a seat across from the Hazari's and leaned forward. "So, what's happening to your friend that's so strange?"

Dr. Hazari introduced himself and asked if Corwin knew of an Ancient Egyptian ring in the shape of a beetle with retractable wings.

Corwin leaned back in his chair and nodded. "So you've found the blasted thing?"

"We didn't," Dr. Hazari said.

"My friend, Jonas Shurmann, found it," Sejal added. "And weird things have been happening ever since."

Corwin frowned. "I was hoping it was gone forever."

"You lost it?" Dr. Hazari asked. "Why didn't you report it missing to the police? You must have it insured."

Corwin shook his head. "Why insure it?" he said. "It goes when and where it wants to go. Always has. Frankly, I was happy to be rid of it. That ring is cursed."

Dr. Hazari shifted in his seat. "Being a man of science, I would normally be skeptical of such a statement, but..." he paused and took a deep breath, "I have seen things that I cannot explain. And I think they may be attributed to your ring."

"The ring doesn't belong to me." Corwin shook his head. "And it doesn't belong to your friend's either. That ring has but one owner: Tutankhamun."

"So it is from the Tut crypt?" Sejal asked.

Corwin nodded. "The man my great-aunt married—Edgar Aldrich—was one clever devil. He built his fortune from trolley cars, hydro-electric power plants, and fruit plantations all by the time he had reached his early forties. Then he and great-aunt Helen retired and spent their days traveling around the world. They took photographs and wrote about all the places they visited for the *New York Times*." Corwin cleared his throat. "I think it was during their travels that they became close friends with Lord Carnarvon—the fifth one, George Herbert. He financed Howard Carter's excavation of King Tut's tomb. And it just so happened that Edgar and Helen decided to visit the dig right when the tomb was discovered. *National Geographic* didn't have anyone there to cover it, so Edgar and Helen filled in. They were the only ones reporting on the greatest archaeological discovery in history. I mean, that was a big deal—the biggest!"

"Wow!" Sejal said. "That was good timing."

Corwin shrugged. "Or bad timing, if you believe in curses."

"Death shall come on swift wings to him who disturbs the peace of the King," Sejal said.

"So, you know it." Corwin gave a weak smile. "Most people who entered that crypt died of old age, but Lord Carnarvon and Edgar and Helen were not among them. Carnarvon died five months later after a mosquito bite on his face became infected. And Edgar and Helen died five years later in Sarajevo."

"How did they die?" Dr. Hazari asked.

"Dad—" Sejal turned to her father.

"It's okay," Corwin assured her. "Edgar took a job as the U.S. Ambassador to Yugoslavia, believe it or not. And Helen was excited about this because she had wanted to write a book about the cultures and customs of the Balkans. So, soon after they arrived, they headed out on their first fact-finding tour of the countryside when—" Corwinn paused and swallowed hard. "There was a terrible accident. Their car ran off the road and tumbled down the side of a mountain."

"Oh, my gosh!" Sejal gasped.

Corwin nodded again. "Somehow the driver walked away without a scratch. But Edgar and Helen were both killed." Slim leaped down from Sejal's lap and went over to Corwin.

"So, how did they end up with the ring, anyway?" Dr. Hazari asked.

"Well, after George Herbert of Carnarvon died, his son, Henry Herbert, became the sixth Lord of Carnarvon, and he invited Edgar and Helen to Highclere Castle, the family home in England." Corwin chuckled. "It's tough keeping track of these royal British guys. Anywho, one night Henry—the *new* Lord Carnarvon—led Edgar and Helen through a secret passage to a concealed chamber. And there, he showed them his father's personal collection from Tut's tomb. Items that were never cataloged by Howard Carter. Treasures that the rest of the world would never see. And from that collection, he gave Helen a ring as a token of his family's friendship."

"Wow!" Dr. Hazari leaned back in his seat. "That's amazing."

Corwin closed his eyes and took a deep breath. "Aunt Helen was wearing it the day of that terrible accident."

Sejal shivered and leaned against her father.

"The ring was mailed back to our family, but no one ever dared to wear it. It was kept locked away." He looked over at the window. "Well, until now."

"Did you at least see who stole it?" Sejal asked.

"All I saw were shadows," Corwin said. Then he nodded his head and added, "And I heard a strange howling noise outside."

Sejal felt her dad shiver.

* * *

Dr. Hazari dropped Sejal off at school the next

morning, then headed over to the Clintonville Co-op for some groceries. He was replaying Corwin Bachert's story in his mind when he spied two familiar figures meandering down the sidewalk on Clintoncrest Avenue. He swung his car up to the curb and jumped out.

"CatBob! Neil—it's me," he called.

The two felines turned and trotted to meet him. He stroked their backs and asked them what they were up to, but the cats only chirped their greetings and purred before turning around to continue on their way.

"Are you two on a case right now?" he asked, following behind. "I don't have a chicken costume, but maybe I can help."

Dr. Hazari took the lack of audible objections as approval and followed the felines down the street. They turned onto Volsung Avenue and then again on East Thurber Road before scampering up the walkway to a green house.

"Okay," Dr. Hazari said, "I guess this is the place." He strode up to the door and knocked.

The door opened and Mr. Shurmann appeared.

"Hey, Dr. Hazari! What's up?"

"To tell you the truth," he said as he pointed to his feline guides, "I'm not sure."

CatBob and Neil rubbed against Mr. Shurmann's

legs before darting past him and up the stairs.

"I just saw them walking down the sidewalk," Dr. Hazari explained, "and decided to tag along to make sure they were okay."

Mr. Shurmann shook his head in wonder. "And they brought you here?"

"Yes. They seemed to know right where they were going."

"Huh. They usually only come over when Jonas is here. This is the first time—" Mr. Shurmann stopped when he saw the cats reemerge at the top of the stairs.

CatBob and Neil were holding Jonas's chicken costume in their teeth.

"That's not right," Mr. Shurmann breathed.

"Why?" Dr. Hazari asked. "Does he always wear those feathers?"

"Pretty much. He would never leave them at home on a school day."

14
SUPERVILLAIN

Jonas felt great. Well, not just great. Jonas felt powerful. He felt *invincible*.

He felt like a giant as he strode through the crowded hallway of George Clinton Elementary. All of the kids and teachers that hustled through the hall around him seemed small somehow, like ants. And he couldn't believe he had ever worried about their opinions of him.

He smiled. His mouth stretched into a wide grin. The grin of a person who doesn't have to worry about what others think. The grin of someone who holds all of the power. Jonas wore the smile of a king.

"Hey, Smiley!" someone called out.

Jonas stopped and turned. Sejal hurried up to him carrying an armload of books.

"Guess who my dad and I talked to last night?"

she sang. "Corwin Bachert! He's the guy who donated the skeletons to the school and..." she leaned in close and whispered, "he's who the scarab ring belongs to."

Jonas narrowed his eyes.

Sejal backed up when she saw the look on his face. "What's wrong?" she asked.

With a deft move, Jonas smacked the books from Sejal's arms, sending them sprawling across the floor. Traffic stopped. Everyone gathered to watch the exchange.

"Hey, Jerkenstein!" Sejal yelled. "What did you do that for?"

"The ring's mine—I found it!" Jonas growled. "And I thought I told you to mind your own business. I don't have time for people that write about fake superheroes."

The crowd of onlookers hooted and laughed.

Sejal bit back the hurt she felt and stepped to Jonas. "I told Corwin you've been a total jerk since you found that thing!" She reached for the ring on Jonas's finger.

Jonas jerked his hand away, then swung it back across Sejal's face. The blow threw her backward into the lockers with a loud *bang!*

The noise shocked the crowd into silence.

"I told you to stay out of my way," Jonas said in

a trembling voice. "I don't need you. I don't need anyone!" He wiped his eyes and turned to leave, but found his way blocked.

"Well, well, well!" Edison smiled the smuggest smile Jonas had ever seen. "Looks like our resident superhero has turned super*villain!*" He grabbed Jonas by the arm.

As Jonas was dragged off, he managed to look back in time to see Danny Martin holding Sejal back as she sprang from the floor.

"Come back here, Jonas Shurmann!" she yelled. "Come back here so I can slap some sense into you!"

A short time later, Jonas was sitting outside the principal's office listening to Edison talk to Mr. Shurmann on the phone.

"Oh, there is no mistake, I assure you, Mr. Shurmann. I personally witnessed Jonas slap that poor girl and knock her to the floor." Edison's voice was almost bubbly as he spoke into the phone. "He isn't going anywhere, but the principal insists on speaking to you and your wife before you take him home. Uh-huh. Yes. Can't wait. Bye-bye."

Jonas wiped tears from his eyes. He couldn't stop crying.

"A little late for crying, isn't it, tough guy?"

Edison said as he stood, lording over Jonas. "Just wait until... then we'll see... you ever again."

Jonas strained to hear what Edison was saying, but his voice seemed to be cutting out.

"What did you say?" Jonas asked, but Edison didn't answer. He disappeared into the principal's office.

Jonas bent over in his seat and held his head in his hands. He must have been crying really hard because his head was throbbing.

He wiped his eyes again. The beetle on his finger knocked into his eye.

"Stupid ring!" he hissed.

He grabbed the stone insect and gave it a tug, but it didn't budge. He gripped it tighter and pulled harder. The band suddenly felt like it was squeezing his finger, which made Jonas panic. If it wouldn't come off, he was certain the doctors would choose to cut his finger off before destroying a priceless ring from Ancient Egypt. But if that's what it took to get the thing off his hand and out of his life, then maybe he would get used to only being able to count to nine on his hands. He just wanted all the craziness to stop, for his life to go back to normal, and to take back everything he had done.

Jonas gritted his teeth. His head was pulsing with sharp pain.

He noticed the principal's assistant was snapping her fingers at him and speaking, but he couldn't hear what she was saying. It was as if she had no voice.

Then Jonas heard a voice that definitely didn't belong to the principal's assistant. It was the same voice he had heard in his dreams and in his room. The same voice that had spoken to him in detention.

It's all right, Jonas, the voice said. *Don't worry. They can't do anything to you. They're all powerless insects.*

The voice soothed him. The throbbing in his head eased.

It's time to go, Jonas, the voice called. *Get up. Let's go.*

Jonas rose from his seat and walked out of the office and down the hall.

He passed his classroom where his classmates sat in their chairs, waiting for Edison to return. He shuffled along he read the "missing" fliers plastered to the walls that offered a reward for the return of the snake skeleton. Then he heard the familiar rattling noise overhead. He followed the sound through the halls until he met a dead end.

Jonas walked to the door marked JANITOR'S CLOSET and pulled the handle.

The room was pitch black inside, but the rattling noise was much louder. Something slithered out of the shadows. Jonas backed away.

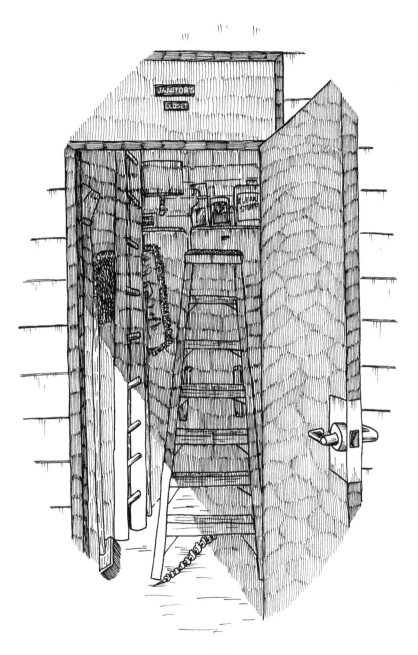

He drew in a sharp breath. "Arthur?" he whispered.

It's time, the voice said. *Time to show them all!*

15
THE SCARAB STRIKES!

"This is so humiliating," Mr. Shurmann said. "I know you just met him, Nirav, but, believe me, Jonas is a good kid." He turned the steering wheel and swung the car into a parking space.

"And I believe he still is," Dr. Hazari said as he stepped out. He looked at the school and shook his head. "It isn't him," he muttered.

"Jonas doesn't make a habit of getting in fights," Mr. Shurmann continued. "My wife and I don't tolerate that kind of behavior."

Dr. Hazari raised a hand to stop him. "It isn't him," he repeated.

"What do you mean, 'it isn't him?'"

"I mean there is more at work here than just your son."

"What? Like drugs?"

"No!" Dr. Hazari waved the suggestion away. "I saw the intruder in my house this weekend, and it wasn't—"

A car horn beeped. Orville's sleek, black car glided to a stop just behind them. The doors swung open and Orville and Tallula stepped out and waved.

"What are you two doing here?" Mr. Shurmann asked.

"We got a call from Sejal at the shop," Orville said. "She said something was seriously wrong, so we got here as fast as we could. What's up?"

"Jonas..." Mr. Shurmann sighed and shook his head.

"Jonas is in trouble," Dr. Hazari said as he hoisted a cat carrier from the back seat. "And he needs his friends. I'm glad Sejal called you."

As soon as they entered the school, Sejal appeared. Her eyes were swollen from crying and she held an ice pack to her face.

Dr. Hazari rushed to her and pulled her close. "What are you doing out here?" he asked.

"Looking for Jonas," she said.

"Looking for Jonas?" Mr. Shurmann said. "The principal told me he's in the office."

Sejal shook her head. "Not any more. Mrs. Johnson, the principal's assistant, said he disappeared, so everyone's looking for him."

"I'm so sorry for what Jonas did, Sejal," Mr. Shurmann said. "I know you must hate him right now, but this isn't like him."

"I know," she said. "And I don't hate Jonas. I'm worried about him."

Sejal led the group down the hall and around a corner, where they encountered a man backing out of a dark room. The man spun around wearing a contemptuous smile on his lips.

"Mr. Shurmann, I'm so glad you're here," Edison exclaimed with an exaggerated heave. "I have never had so much trouble with a student as I have had with Jonas."

"So where is he?" Mr. Shurmann asked.

"It would seem he's hiding from his punishment," Edison said, "and holding up our sneak peek of the new skeleton exhibit."

"You must be Edison," Orville started.

"Tomb," the teacher sang as he offered his hand. "I'm covering for Miss Keys while she's out sick."

Mr. Shurmann handed the shopping bag he'd been carrying to Sejal, grabbed Edison's slender hand, and squeezed.

Edison gritted his teeth under Mr. Shurmann's vice grip. "Ahhh. Pleased to meet you," he squeaked.

Mr. Shurmann yanked on Edison's hand, pulling him closer. His nose twitched as he sniffed foul air, then he glared at the teacher through his hexagonal eyeglass frames and growled. "So you're telling me you lost my son?"

"Of course not." Edison whimpered as he struggled to free his hand. "He's still here—somewhere—and we'll see to it that he's found and punished."

"Jonas is missing?!" a voice echoed from behind the group.

Mrs. Shurmann marched up to Edison with her tattooed arms folded. "I'm Jonas's mother," she announced. "I got a call saying Jonas was in the office. How did he escape? Was no one watching him?"

"No," Tallula whispered. "They apparently just let him walk out."

"No one *let* him walk out," Edison snapped. "There's no controlling that boy. He's wandering the halls, hitting people, and now he's—"

Edison stopped. His attention was suddenly focused on a shrill scream coming from around the corner.

Everyone listened as more screams followed. The squeak of sneakers on waxed floors joined the chorus. Kids were running—a lot of kids.

Mr. Shurmann pushed past Edison and headed toward the commotion. As he rounded the corner he was pushed against the wall by a mob of stampeding children.

"Whoa!" he said, stopping a passing boy. "What's going on?"

The boy gazed up at Mr. Shurmann with wild eyes. "There's a monster in the atrium, and it's got Jonas Shurmann!"

Mr. Shurmann instructed the boy to lead the other children to a fire exit and called to his wife and the others to follow him.

By the time they reached the atrium, it was empty and dark. In the center, three towers of scaffolds stood arranged in a *U*, around a small stage that held the skeleton exhibit.

"What has he done now?" Edison asked, looking around.

Orville and Talulla heard hissing coming from the cat carriers they held. Orville lifted his and peeked in.

"What's up, Neil," he asked.

The cyclopean feline pawed at the carrier door and cried.

"I think they want out," he said as he sat the carrier on the floor and released the detective. He nodded to Talulla to do the same.

"I'm going to have to insist you keep—" Edison began. But his words withered in his mouth when he caught the expression on Mr. Shurmann's face.

CatBob and Neil sprang from their carriers and

scanned the cavernous room, raising their heads and sniffing at the air. They sniffed toward Edison and hissed in unison, then turned their attention to the scaffolds.

"What is it, guys?" Orville asked, crouching beside them. "What do you smell?"

The cats whined and trotted toward the stage.

"I know you're used to being at a vet's office, but this is a learning institution," Edison said. "Letting animals run free is against school policy."

"I'm sure losing students is, too," Mrs. Shurmann fired back.

"I think they smell something," Orville said as he followed behind the two detectives. "I just wish I knew what it was."

"Maybe you can ask them," Mr. Shurmann said. He motioned to Sejal. "Give Orville the bag."

She tossed the plastic shopping bag over. Orville thrust his hand into it and drew out a mass of white feathers. He turned to Mr. Shurmann. "He isn't wearing his feathers?"

Dr. Hazari shook his head. "It was our first clue that something was wrong."

"Oh, please!" Edison laughed. "You actually believe all of that chicken costume nonsense? No wonder your son is living in a fantasy world—you're enabling him!"

"And I suppose all of the students we saw running from here were scared off by a fantasy?" Dr. Hazari asked.

"The boy I stopped said there was a monster in here and it had Jonas," Mr. Shurmann said.

"Well, hopefully CatBob and Neil can tell us something," Orville put in as he pulled the feathers over his wild Afro. He held it in place while Tallula and Sejal tied the sleeves under his chin. When they had finished, Orville turned around and presented himself. "How do I look?"

"Ridiculous," Mr. Shurmann said. "Does it work? Can you hear the cats?"

Orville crouched low as he crept toward the scaffolding. "It needs washed, that's for sure," he whispered. He scanned the stage and spotted the felines, jumping up on one of the scaffold towers. "CatBob, Neil, where are you going?" he called.

"To save Jonas," CatBob said.

"Holy crap!" Orville exclaimed. "I just heard you talk!"

"Shhh!" Neil spat. "It can hear you."

Orville winced. "Sorry. What can hear me?"

Neil looked up at the adjoining scaffold. Orville followed his gaze to two blue lights that hovered in the darkness.

"Well, what should we do?" Orville whispered.

"Get Jonas down from there while it's fighting us," CatBob answered.

"And get that ring away from him!" Neil added.

With that, the cats made a few quick leaps upward and disappeared into the shadows.

Orville motioned for the others to approach. As he did, a terrible racket erupted. Hissing, screaming, and a weird rattling noise that sounded like something stuck in the spokes of a spinning bicycle wheel echoed through the rafters overhead.

"Where is Jonas?" Mr. Shurmann asked.

"He's up in the scaffolding," Orville said, pointing to the blue lights that were now bobbing and weaving in the gloom. "CatBob and Neil are fighting something up there—whatever those blue lights are."

"It's a snake," Dr. Hazari said. "At least the bones of one."

"Arthur?" Edison asked. "The missing snake bones? How did they get up there?"

"Someone needs to climb up there to bring Jonas down," Dr. Hazari said. "Sejal, wait!" He motioned to his daughter to get off of the scaffolds, but she was already hoisting herself up the steel poles, disappearing into the darkness above.

The adults scanned the shadows, nervously watching for a sign, but the gloom concealed everything from view except for the two blue lights. They continued to weave wildly. They darted to an adjoining tower and the hisses and screams intensified.

"Now!" Orville heard Neil yell.

Orville relayed the signal into the darkness overhead.

Then the two blue lights flared. A blue fireball exploded with a loud *whoosh!* The light revealed the missing snake skeleton wrapped around the steel poles of the scaffolding. The top half weaved wildly to avoid CatBob and Neil Higgins as they lunged at the bones with claws and teeth bared. The human skull atop the spine was engulfed in blue fire. And on the adjoining tower, they spotted Sejal helping Jonas onto one of the wooden platforms. "Stay back, Arthur!" Sejal squealed as the snake skeleton turned its glowing head toward her.

"Hurry, guys!" Tallula yelled from below.

But before Sejal and Jonas could escape, Arthur weaved through the poles with lightning speed and coiled itself around Jonas.

Fireballs shot from the eye sockets, sending Sejal stumbling backward. She caught herself on a pole just before tumbling over the edge.

The flames contracted into two pinpoints of light as the snake weaved its way upward, disappearing into the darkness with Jonas held in its ribcage. An eerie

silence settled over the room as the cats gave chase into the void. The onlookers stared upward, into the black, waiting for some sign. Then, a burst of blue flame lit up the room.

CatBob and Neil dropped down upon the monster and renewed their assault. An empty scream echoed through the atrium as a shower of bone fragments rained down onto the adults below.

Arthur released Jonas and sprang at its attackers. Jonas struggled to his feet and lowered himself over the edge of the platform. He called to Sejal, who began climbing up toward him.

"Hold on, Jonas!" she called. "I'm almost there."

"Hurry!" Jonas cried, "I can't hold—" His hand slipped from the pole and he fell.

For two seconds, Jonas twisted in the air.

His dad leaped forward, arms outstretched to catch him.

Just before he reached his dad's arms, a loud *pong!* resounded through the atrium. The noise echoed from the high ceiling and faded as Mr. Shurmann gently laid Jonas on the floor. "I gotcha, Bud," he said. "You're okay."

Jonas's eyes didn't open.

"Jonas?" Mrs. Shurmann cried. She shook him, but his eyes remained closed. She bent down and put her ear to his mouth.

No one moved.

"What's wrong with him?" Edison asked.

"He's not breathing," Mrs. Shurmann said.

16
TWILIGHT WORLD

Jonas opened his eyes. The world had gone silent. The sickening reverberation of his head striking the steel pole had stopped. The screeching of his cat-friends and the rattling of Arthur's bones was gone as well.

As he rose, he saw strange, dark figures hovering over him. A scream caught in his throat as the specters closed in, forming a canopy of ghostly shade, then one of them drifted away out of sight.

At first, Jonas thought the figures were shadows, but he saw no one else around that could be casting them. With a trembling hand, he reached out to touch one.

His hand passed right through it.

He scrambled to his feet, crept out of the shade, and was relieved when the figures didn't follow him.

The school atrium looked just as it had only moments ago during the chaos, yet Jonas could tell it was somehow different. The strange tension that had filled the air had been replaced by an eerie silence that was suddenly disturbed by a single, far-off meow.

Jonas strained his ears and followed the sound to the main hallway, where a small, orange cat emerged from around the corner at the opposite end. It looked at him and let out another distressed cry.

The familiar sight of the feline made Jonas feel better. "Hey, little guy," he called. "What are you doing in here? Are you lost?"

Then, the cat turned and crouched. It spat hisses at two large shadows that stretched out from behind the corner. The feline backed away, then darted across the passage and out of sight. Jonas took off in pursuit.

"What's wrong? Don't go!" he called.

A terrible growl boomed through the hall. Jonas slowed his pace as two wolves stalked into view.

"Hey!" Jonas yelled as he renewed his charge toward them. "Leave him alone!"

The wolves eyed Jonas for a moment before turning their attention back to the cat. With a single leap, they disappeared from view, after their prey.

Jonas pumped his legs and flew around the corner. He saw the wolves ahead of him, quickly closing in on the frightened cat. The feline cut right and Jonas followed down a parallel hall. He knew the school's hallways by heart and knew his new cat-friend was headed for a dead end.

As he reached the end of the hall, the cat reap-peared, sliding to stop just short of the block wall. Jonas slid to a stop right in front of it.

The wolves lunged. Jagged teeth rushed toward Jonas as he crouched over the trembling cat and held it to his chest.

Jonas gritted his teeth and winced, bracing for the savage bites of the beasts, but nothing happened. He raised his head and looked around. The hall was empty. He sat up and looked down at the cat, who peered up in turn with wide eyes.

Meow.

Jonas scooped up the cat and it dissolved into grains of sand that ran through his fingers and scat-tered on the floor.

"Oh, no!" he cried. He bent down and attempted to gather the sand, but a sudden gust whipped though the hallway, and took with it every trace of the cat.

"Why did you do that?" a voice boomed from behind him.

Jonas looked over his shoulder and saw someone hobbling toward him at the far end of the hall. As the figure neared, Jonas saw its left foot was turned sharply inward at the ankle, causing the side of the foot to touch the floor.

"Why would you sacrifice yourself to save a child of Bast?" the figure demanded.

"I'm a friend to all cats," Jonas declared. "The wolves were bigger and there were two of them. It wasn't fair!"

The man limped forward, emerging from the shadows. He straightened up and looked down his nose at Jonas.

Jonas saw the man was actually a boy—a teenager, with a round, shaved head. His dark eyes held Jonas with narrowed suspicion. He wore only a white *shenti*, or linen kilt, around his waist.

"Such valor will not go unpunished in this place," the boy said. Jonas could see the boy's front teeth stuck out, affecting his speech. That, or he had an accent Jonas had never heard before. It was difficult to tell.

Suddenly the pair heard gruff voices behind them. The boy grabbed Jonas firmly by the shoulder, then waved his hand and muttered some strange-sounding words. "Do not move or make a sound," he whispered.

Two figures appeared at the end of the hall. They were tall, slender figures, with big heads. As they drew closer, Jonas saw they were actually men clad

in black *shentis* with bands of bronze on their arms and wrists. But what frightened Jonas most were their masks. Each man's face was concealed behind a black metal jackal head.

The jackalheads slowed as they approached the dead end where Jonas and the boy stood with their backs pressed against the wall. The men scanned the lockers as if they couldn't see Jonas or the boy, but were looking for them. After a few moments, one grunted something incomprehensible. Both jackalheads drew sickle-shaped swords and held ready as they stepped forward.

Jonas pressed back into the bricks as hard as he could but couldn't get any flatter. He held his breath as a metal jackal snout stopped just inches from his face. There was a moment of silence, then more incomprehensible words came from under the helmet. Both men lowered their swords and quickly retreated.

As soon as they had disappeared around the corner, Jonas took a big gulp of air. "How come they couldn't see us?" he asked.

"An illusion. Just like the cat and the wolves," the boy answered.

"Who were those guys?"

"Slaves of Ramose II. Men forced to search this city for eternity until they find what they were sent to capture."

"What are they looking for?"

"Me," came the reply.

"Where are we?" Jonas asked, looking around. "I know it looks like my school, but there's something about it that seems..." He reached out and touched one of the walls. "Fake," he added. "Like we're in a dream."

The boy nodded. "Very observant." He waved his hand and the lockers and painted cinderblock walls of George Clinton Elementary vanished. Jonas looked around in amazement. They were suddenly standing outside, in a narrow alley that cut between buildings that were covered in crumbling white plaster. Jonas began to speak, but paused when he saw the boy raise his head as if listening to something far away. The boy lifted his walking stick and pointed to the end of the alley. "We must keep moving," he said.

Jonas watched the boy stride off. He wasn't sure if he should trust this stranger, but the boy seemed much friendlier than the jackalheads. Plus, Jonas had no idea where he was or how to find a way back home. "Lead the way," he sighed as he jogged up beside his mysterious guide.

The mouth of the alley opened into a maze of dusty, winding passages that all looked the same. And despite the boy's clubfoot, he navigated the labyrinth with surprising agility. Jonas had trouble keeping up.

The pair emerged on a crowded street, lined with merchant carts. People clustered together, pushing their way to the front of the crowd, to arguing over the quality and price of the wares. The scent of exotic spices and burning wood hung in the hazy air. But Jonas noticed something odd about everyone he saw as he made his way through the bazaar. They wore sad expressions and stood with slouched shoulders.

"They're all prisoners here," the boy said, reading Jonas's expression. "I was the first. This city was created to hold me for all eternity."

"All eternity? How long have you been here?" Jonas asked as he spotted two jackalheads emerging from the crowd just ahead. Before he could alert his guide, the boy pulled him into a darkened doorway.

"4,660 years," the boy whispered.

"What?"

"You asked how long I've been here. This will be my 4,660th year." The boy peeked around the corner, then led Jonas back into the crowd, where they continued snaking their way through the market. "A curse was placed on my tomb," he continued. "And not just an empty threat carved on my crypt to deter thieves, but a real curse. Anyone who has taken something of mine has been struck down and sent here."

Jonas looked up at the boy. "The scarab ring— that was yours?" he asked.

The boy turned and nodded.

Jonas didn't know what to say. He looked at his new friend, awestruck.

"There is but one way of escape," the boy added.

Just as Jonas was about to ask what that was, someone grabbed his arm. He tried to pull free, but the grip was too strong. He screamed as one of the jackalheads yanked him off his feet and began dragging him back through the crowd.

The boy lunged at Jonas's attacker, ramming the end of his walking stick into the jackalhead's helmet. The sentry went tumbling backward into the dust. Jonas broke free and saw two more jackalheads charging through the crowd toward them.

The boy reached into a pouch in his *shenti* and flung a handful of coins at the downed jackalhead. The crowd erupted into chaos as bystanders dove for the coins. The sentries were lost in the ensuing melee as people punched, kicked, and clawed to wrest the treasure away from one another.

The boy pulled Jonas away from the pandemonium and into an alley.

"Thanks, Tut— I mean..." Jonas stopped himself,

just in case he wasn't dreaming and his new friend actually was King Tut. Jonas thought it best to address the Pharaoh by his full name. He was a king, after all. But Jonas didn't know the proper way to address him as he hadn't had much experience talking to kings.

The boy stopped and spun around, grabbing Jonas with his free hand. "I am Tutankhamun," he thundered, "Pharaoh of the New Kingdom, the living image of Amun, and son of Akhenaten."

"I— I'm sorry," Jonas stammered. "Uh, King— I mean…" Jonas stopped when he saw the boy's expression soften and a hint of a smile pass his lips.

"I jest, my friend!" the King said as he released Jonas. "I understand your people call me Tut now."

"Wow," Jonas whispered. "I'm Jonas. Jonas Shurmann."

"Formality has no place here, Jonas. We are all equally prisoners of Ramose, which is why we must keep moving. I suspect the villain is beginning to realize he has been tricked."

As the pair made their way farther into another maze, Jonas spoke up. "Who is this Ramose guy, anyway, and why did he trap you here in the first place?"

"In life, he was the son of Ramose I, and a very influential man who served as grand vizier of Upper

Egypt under my father, Akhenaten, and my grandfather, Amenhotep III. Ramose I was also the governor of Thebes and the high priest of the cult of Aten. It was he who persuaded my father to issue a royal decree stating Aten was the only god to be worshipped in the empire. I never liked Ramose and I liked his son even less. Ramose II is a power-mad buffoon who lacks his father's intelligence and political savvy. Thankfully he never became grand vizier, but he did inherit his father's office as high priest. So when I became pharaoh, I banned the cult of Aten. I believe people should worship as they choose...and I didn't want Ramose holding influence over the throne. The ban stripped Ramose of his political power. He swore revenge, of course."

Tut's mouth stretched into a rueful smile and he shook his head. "I was made Pharaoh of the greatest empire on the planet when I was scarcely older than you, Jonas. I was too young to bear such responsibility, so I appointed my uncle, Ay, to maintain law until I was ready to rule, and he did very well. However, once I came of age, Ay decided he didn't want to give up the throne. After I banned Atenism, Ramos and Ay conspired together and had me murdered."

Tut gritted his teeth as he spoke. "And after we die, we Egyptians have far to travel in death. We must journey through a frightening place called the

Duat to reach the Hall of Two Truths, where our hearts are weighed against the Feather of Truth. And if we pass, we are reunited with our families."

"What happens if you don't pass?" Jonas asked.

"A terrible monster called the Devourer eats us. Which is why many in this city do not wish to leave."

"But you said there is a way out of here," Jonas said.

Tut nodded. "Possibly. The arena."

Jonas shivered. Goosebumps rose on his skin. He felt like his sweatshirt was suddenly paper-thin. He rubbed his arms and looked up at the sky to see if the weather was changing or if night was falling. The brightest moon he had ever seen hung overhead, but the sky was still blue as if it were night and day at the same time. "I'm getting cold," he said.

Tut placed a hand on Jonas's shoulder. "I'm sorry, Jonas, but it would appear that in the Land of the Living, you've stopped breathing."

Jonas backed away. "You mean I'm dead?"

Tut nodded.

"But I can get back, right?" Jonas began to panic. "There has to be a way to get back to the Land of the Living. You said it was the arena, right?"

"Very possibly," Tut said. "But it will depend on you. For now we must keep moving." He turned and led Jonas down another crooked alley. "If we are captured, there may be no way back."

17

THE ARENA

Jonas stayed close to Tut as they made their way through the winding web of alleyways that criss-crossed the streets and thoroughfares. The pair moved quickly, only pausing at major intersections to look for jackalheads among the sad faces.

As they neared the center of the city, sudden roars from a cheering crowd periodically drowned out the sounds of everyday life. The pair watched from the safety of the shadows as the city's inhabitants filed silently toward a hulking structure ahead of them.

"Every night the prisoners gather in the arena to watch...and to fight," Tut whispered.

"Why?" Jonas asked.

"It is the only distraction from their torment," Tut answered. "And some believe it's their only chance to escape."

The pair darted across a street into the opposite alleyway.

"So how can I get back to the Land of the Living?" Jonas whispered.

"The only way is to defeat Ramose in the arena," Tut replied.

"Why haven't you done it already?" Jonas asked. "You knocked that jackal-man down when he grabbed me. Why not sneak up to Ramose and give him a smack with the old walking stick? Then you'd be on your way to the Hall of Justice."

"It's the Hall of Two Truths," Tut corrected him. "And I'm afraid it isn't quite as simple as you make it out to be—especially when you have this." He pointed to his clubfoot. "Ramose created this city with very powerful magic, and in this realm, his power is unrivaled. I wasn't fit for chariot races when I was breathing. Ramose would make short work of me here, and he knows it. That's why his challenge has stood unanswered for more than 4,000 years." Tut frowned at Jonas and shook his head. "The only way I've managed to avoid capture has been by hiding in the alleys behind illusions."

They crept to the end of the alley and Tut pointed to a stone structure that rose high above the rooftops in the moonlight. Jonas could see people standing at the very top edge. The figures rose from their seats in time with the deafening roars that came from the other side of the stone walls.

"That's Ramose's arena," Tut said. "After a thousand years of failing to capture me, he issued a new challenge. He decreed that I could choose a warrior to fight in my place."

"So why didn't you just wait for a really big guy to show up and have him punch Ramose in his stupid face?"

"I thought about that very thing for a long time," Tut said. "Centuries, actually. And such a man eventually arrived here. But when I spoke to him, I realized why I could not choose him."

"Why?" Jonas asked.

"Because his character wasn't up to the task. In those days, only thieves and cutthroats appeared. That's how he ended up here." Tut sighed. "I realized then that Ramose's new challenge was a clever one. It was a test of my wisdom and my patience just as much as it was a test of the heart of the chosen warrior—three-fold the difficulty of his initial challenge."

Tut led Jonas behind a row of buildings directly across from the arena's entrance, where they found a vantage point from which to watch.

"Then a strange thing happened," Tut continued. "Suddenly, a different sort of prisoner began appearing: learned scholars who spend their lives studying Egypt and my life."

"Yeah," Jonas said. "Edgar and Helen Aldrich must be here! Have you seen them?"

Tut nodded. "The Aldriches are very good people. Very much a different breed from the miscreants I had been used to seeing. They taught me much about how Egypt's contributions continued in other nations. It was when I met the Aldriches that I recognized my chance to fool Ramose—which is why I guided you to the ring. You followed my map."

Jonas was taken aback by this news. "You were the hand in the sand?" he asked.

Tut flashed a mischievous grin. "I'm stubborn, too. I knew warning you about the ring would only draw you to it and further into Ramose's design. I prayed for him to make the mistake I have been waiting for."

"What mistake is that?"

"Capturing a warrior instead of a dishonorable thief or a curious scholar," Tut said. "When Ramose spoke to you, he preyed upon your need to feel special. But I believe he has completely underestimated you, and that gives you an advantage."

Jonas frowned. "The talking snake skeleton was Ramose?"

Tut nodded.

Jonas hung his head. "Sorry, Tut, but I think Ramose is right. I thought I was a hero, once, but not anymore. I was a total jerk to my best friends, Cat-Bob and Neil, and I hit Sejal when she was trying to save me from the ring." He stopped and stared at the boy-king. "Besides, I can't fight an adult in an arena. Look at me; I'm just a kid. I don't even have my feathers."

Tut looked at Jonas sympathetically. "Come on, we're almost there."

"One good thing about living in a city of thieves," Tut said as he hobbled ahead into a shaft of light, "you can find a tunnel to just about anywhere you want to go."

Jonas and Tut had spied on the crowds that gathered at the arena's entrance from the alley. The company of Ramose's jackalheads they watched stop and frisk every person in line crushed Jonas's hopes of ever getting in. But Tut only smiled and motioned for Jonas to follow him.

The boy-king led him through the door to one of the buildings they had been hiding behind. Inside, he opened a small closet and lifted a rug that covered the floor. Jonas gasped. The rug revealed a hole in the floor that led into a tunnel. Tut explained that the passage ran under the street and into the arena. They donned linen robes to diguise themselves and climbed down the ladder.

Jonas could tell when they had reached the arena because he could actually feel the vibrations from the cheers of the crowd overhead.

Jonas helped Tut up the ladder on the other end and the pair were soon mixed in among the hordes of spectators shuffling up the stairs to their seats.

They emerged in the moonlight near the very top. Jonas paused and looked over the capacity crowd. People stood, pumping their fists in the air and cheering as a barbaric battle raged in the sand below. Jonas tapped Tut on the shoulder as he led the way down the steps.

"Hey, Tut," Jonas whispered, "are you still angry at all of these people for stealing your treasure?"

Tut smiled. "No," he answered without hesitation. "I have lived among thieves for a very long time, and it has taught me that desperation often forces good people to commit bad deeds." Then he leaned in and looked Jonas in the eye and added, "And I have lost all desire for wealth. All the gold in the world cannot make a man truly rich."

A few moments later, Tut directed Jonas to two open seats mid-way down in the central column. The seats were actually long, stone blocks with wooden planks laid on top. Hardly cushy, but Jonas was exhausted from running and hiding. He flopped down and took in the gruesome spectacle unfolding on the sand below.

Two jackalheads squared off in the center of the arena. The crowd cheered as one of the sentries drove his bo staff into the gut of his opponent. Jonas watched as the injured man quickly grabbed the end of his challenger's staff and fell forward upon it.

The pole snapped in two with a loud *crack!*

The fallen man then leaped to his feet with the broken end in hand and unleashed a flurry of blows upon his stunned and unarmed adversary. A thunderous roar went up as his opponent's body fell limply into the sand.

"Did he kill that guy?!" Jonas asked Tut.

"One cannot die in this realm as we died in the Land of the Living," the boy-king explained, "but a spirit can be defeated—even broken—which can be worse than physical death. However the winner's test is not over. His final challenger is much more powerful and will test the very will of his heart as well as his brawn. That's where all challengers have failed." Tut motioned to the far end of the arena, where a small stone stage stood. Under a cloth canopy, a man dressed in a gold shenti leaped from a throne and raised his arms. The crowd responded with another thunderous cheer.

"We have a new challenger!" the man bellowed. His voice was so loud that Jonas could hear it clearly over the audience's applause. "One who's thirst for freedom outweighs his fear. A man brave enough to accept a challenge that even a king has cowered from for more than 4,000 years."

A burst of light exploded from the platform, forcing onlookers to shield their eyes. A gasp swept through the stands. A moment later, the man in the gold *shenti* reappeared in the center of the arena, clad in golden armor. He gripped a golden staff in his fist as he addressed the crowd.

"That is Ramose," Tut whispered in Jonas's ear.

"May your journey through the Duat be swift and your heart be judged worthy!" the priest said as he spun his staff like a helicopter propeller. "Let the battle begin!" he shouted into the stands.

The crowd rose to their feet as the jackalhead squared off with his master. The sentry lunged, thrusting his staff at a terrific speed, but Ramose dodged so quickly, Jonas didn't actually see him move. The jackalhead struck again, undaunted. Again and again he delivered a series of short, powerful thrusts that would have easily crippled anyone caught in their path. But no matter how fast or how precise the attack, each one failed to find its target.

Ramose retaliated by landing a series of sharp

strikes to the jackalhead's back and sides. Then he spread his arms wide to taunt his opponent for the audience's amusement. Laughter spilled from the stands. The sentry advanced again, thrusting his staff. Another miss, but this time, the jackalhead spun around, swinging the staff wide as he whirled. Ramose materialized to the jackalhead's side just as the staff came around.

Crack!

The priest staggered backward, dazed from the sharp blow to the face. The crowd fell silent. Ramose's opponent didn't hesitate. He thrust his staff into his opponent's stomach, folding Ramose in half.

Jonas leaped to his feet and cheered as Ramose collapsed to the ground.

"Yeah! Go, Jackal-Man!" he shouted. "Give that big jerk-a-saurus a taste of his own medicine."

Tut grabbed Jonas by the shoulder and forced him to his seat. "Stop that," the king hissed. "You'll expose us!"

"Ramose wasn't fighting fair!" Jonas whispered. "He's a cheater!"

The outburst caused the jackalhead to pause and search the stands for the source of the cheering. When he turned his attention back to his opponent, Ramose had already risen to his feet.

The priest raised his hand and a bolt of lightning

leaped from his palm, sending the jackalhead flying across the arena. The sentry smashed against the stone wall and fell into a crumpled heap in the sand. He did not get up.

Ramose scanned the silent stands. "Who dares root against me?" he demanded. Just as before, the priest's voice boomed through the arena and echoed into the city. "Show yourself, dog, and face the consequences!"

Murmurs trickled through the crowd.

Tut turned to Jonas. "I'm afraid you have forced our hand."

"I didn't mean to," Jonas whispered.

"No matter. I suppose the time has come," Tut said as he climbed up on the wooden planks and peeled back the hood of his robe. "I root against you, Ramose!" he shouted.

18
ROYAL
RUMBLE

"Do my eyes deceive me? Does the brat-king finally grace us with his presence?" Ramose sneered.

"I have selected a champion, Ramose!" Tut announced.

"Who?!" the priest boomed. He vanished and reappeared standing on the blocks of the row above Tut. "Where is this champion? Show him to me!"

Tut turned to Jonas.

Ramose roared with laughter. "After four thousand years you've decided to wager your freedom—and that of every soul here—on this petulant child?" He looked out over the disbelieving faces in the crowd and laughed again. "I must admit, Tutankhamun, I have always doubted your wisdom, but I would have never dared to dream you would make a choice as absurd as this." He raised his arms to the onlookers and bellowed. "What say you?"

The crowd responded with boos and jeers.

Ramose laughed. "To battle, then!"

A company of jackalheads escorted Jonas and Tut to the holding pen while the arena floor was cleared of bodies and debris.

Tut leaned over and whispered to Jonas. "My life and my rule as Pharaoh was short. There were so many things I never got to do for my people. I wanted to be a great king, like Tutmoses III, but my chance to be a wise king has long past. However," he said as he gripped Jonas's shoulder, "I still have this final chance to be a wise man. I can choose the warrior with the power to defeat Ramose and release me so that I can face the challenges of the Duat and the Hall of Two Truths."

"But I allowed the ring to change me. I treated everyone like a jerk," Jonas said in a strained voice.

"Ramose's words clouded your perception, and his influence caused you to act like a fool. But if your love for your family and friends still remains, then he has changed nothing," Tut said. "You are still a hero!"

"Yeah, maybe." Jonas nodded.

The iron portcullis before them raised and Jonas and Tut were shoved into the arena. All around them, the audience leaned over the stone wall to hurl words of abuse. They shook their fists and screamed curses. Amid this chaos, Jonas noticed a man and woman sitting still amid the chaos, looking upon Tut with pleading expressions.

"Who are they?" Jonas asked, pointing to them.

"Edgar and Helen Aldrich," the boy-king replied. "It would appear even those who revere me doubt my wisdom today."

A vortex of gray smoke shot from the floor of the arena and swirled upward. Ramose swaggered out of the wispy tendrils and strutted around the arena, twirling his staff in his fingers, and flashing a cocky grin. The crowd leaped to their feet and cheered.

"Ramose is way too powerful," Jonas said as he watched his opponent peacock for the crowd. "He has armor and he knows magic. All I have are jeans and a sweatshirt. I don't even have my chicken costume. I don't want to let you down, but there's no way I can beat that guy."

"I've been watching matches in this arena for over forty centuries," Tut said. "And I've learned that muscle doesn't make might in this realm. Just like Ramose, you are much more powerful in this world."

"How do you mean?" Jonas asked.

"Your chicken costume didn't make you a hero,"

Tut said. "It's what you did with it that made you a hero. Your deeds were heroic and your reasons were noble. When you fight here, your honor and humility will be your power. Do you understand?"

Jonas frowned. "Maybe."

"But you must be very careful, Jonas." Tut kneeled down. "Even though Ramose cannot harm your physical body here, he can break your spirit and bind you to this realm forever."

"Enough talk!" Ramose bellowed.

Tut struggled to his feet and squeezed Jonas's shoulder. "Allow him to think he's won, then attack like a lion," he whispered before sentries surrounded him and escorted him to the stone stage.

When Jonas turned back, a wooden bo staff appeared in front of him and hung in the air. As soon as he reached for it, the weapon dropped into the sand at his feet. Laughter rippled through the stands as he bent down to retrieve it.

The staff felt much heavier than he had anticipated. He wondered how he would even be able to swing it fast enough to hit Ramose. Then he felt something bite his knuckles and he dropped the staff.

Crack!

Jonas's fingers hurt so bad that the pain took his breath away. He waved his hands as tears rolled down his cheeks. Ramose stood lording over him, his face

twisted in disgust.

"Pathetic!" the priest snarled.

When Jonas regained his breath, he dove for his weapon, but Ramose's staff caught him in the chest, sending him tumbling backward into the sand.

The arena walls resounded with roars of approval.

When Jonas finally managed to suck air into his lungs, a sharp chill ran though his body.

Tut's wrong, he thought. *I'm not going to get out of here. And CatBob and Neil are going to be left alone with no one to help them solve mysteries and save cats. And it's all because I didn't appreciate them.*

Jonas gulped a big breath and gritted his teeth. Never seeing his best friends again suddenly hurt worse than his hands and his chest. He stumbled to his feet and scanned the sand for his staff. In a flash, Ramose appeared before him. Jonas flung sand into the priest's face and dove between his legs, then scrambled across the arena for his weapon. He grabbed the staff and rolled to his feet.

Ramose spun around, wiping the grit from his face, and smiled. Then he was gone. Without thinking, Jonas swung his staff around in a circle as hard as he could.

Ramose reappeared in the staff's path.
Crack!

The sound from the impact echoed through the stands. Ramose staggered backward, furious and humiliated.

But the sharp jolt that transferred through the staff hurt Jonas's hands and the spin made him dizzy. He dropped the staff and fell face-first into the sand. When he regained his bearings, he scrambled to his feet and tried to pull the staff from the sand, but it wouldn't budge. Ramose's armored foot pinned it in place.

Jonas braced for the priest's attack but Ramose didn't move. He just stood there looking at Jonas in disbelief.

"What is this?" Ramose yelled across the arena to the stone stage where Tut stood surrounded by jackalheads.

The pharaoh remained silent.

Jonas looked down and saw that his arm was covered in white feathers. His jeans and sweatshirt were gone. He was wearing his chicken costume! A smile crossed his lips.

Crack!

Something smashed into Jonas's face. His head spun and he staggered backward as Ramose's staff collided with his ribs, his arms, and finally his knee. He shrieked in agony as his leg gave out and he toppled to the floor. Jonas writhed in the dust as a sickening chill shot through his body. He hugged himself in an attempt to ease the bite of the cold.

Once the frigid shock began to subside, Jonas caught his breath and rolled over. He discovered his cries were the only sounds echoing from the stone walls. Ramose stood in the middle of the arena, glaring at the silent spectators, but every eye in the stands was locked on Jonas.

Jonas didn't know why, but he was too cold to care. He was freezing. His teeth chattered as he struggled to rise. Then Sejal popped into his mind: how nice she and her dad had been to him and his friends and how terribly he had treated her. He rubbed his face where Ramose's staff had struck him. Sejal must have felt just like this when he had hit her. He wiped his face with his sleeve and began limping across the arena toward the priest.

Ramose stepped back as Jonas approached. For a moment, the two warriors just stood staring at one another, then Jonas lifted his staff from the sand. Ramose took advantage of his opponent's vulnerable position and lunged, but his attack met an abrupt stop when Jonas caught Ramose's weapon in his bare hand. A collective gasp shot through the crowd.

"Impossible!" the priest gasped.

Jonas lifted his staff from the floor and swung it with amazing speed. The strike lifted Ramose off his feet and sent him flying into the arena wall. The impact sent an enormous cloud of dust over the stands. A few uncertain moments passed while the haze settled. Jonas reemerged to the crowd shifting in their seats, murmuring to one another, and pointed at him.

Jonas looked down and discovered that his chicken feathers had turned into solid metal. He ran his hand down the scale mail armor that covered his chest. Even his staff had turned into metal, but to his surprise, it didn't feel any heavier. And best of all, he didn't feel cold anymore.

Jonas looked across the arena to Ramose, who was on his feet again, twirling his staff in his fingers. The priest drove the end of the pole into the sand and the ground shook.

The arena floor rolled and opened up. The sand under Jonas's feet began to sink out of sight. The vanishing grains revealed a jagged chasm that yawned open like a giant mouth. Jonas was thrown sideways into the sand. Before he could recover, Ramose was upon him.

"How dare you challenge my power!" the villain screamed. He turned to the stands and beheld the crowd with narrowed eyes. "This is what will happen if any of you dogs dare to challenge me again!" He brought his staff down across Jonas's shoulders.

Jonas collapsed onto the floor and curled into a ball as the priest's armored foot delivered a flurry of sharp kicks and stomps. Then Ramose clutched Jonas by the throat and hoisted him to his feet.

"You are all mine—forever!" he roared. "Especially you, Tutankhamun. You will suffer eternity serving as my savage amusement in this arena. Say goodbye to your so-called champion."

With that, Ramose placed his palm to Jonas's chest and a bolt of lightning burst forth, launching Jonas into the arena wall in a flash.

The wall buckled under the force of the impact, sending another cloud of dust and debris into the stands. A large chunk of stone broke loose and tumbled into the sand.

The lights went out.

Jonas felt like he was being buried under ice. The chill bit into him with a ferocity he had never before experienced, but despite the pain, he could only think of one thing...

His mom and dad.

They had no idea how far away he was or what he was going through. He imagined how hurt they would be if he never came back to them.

The thought made Jonas shudder. He was suddenly wracked with pain far worse than the cold. He felt as though his chest had been torn open, and the wound filled by the darkness that surrounded him.

Jonas's heart had broken.

"Boo!" Distant jeers came from the very top rows.

"Silence!" Ramose barked.

As the cloud of dust filled the stands, more voices joined in. Soon, the entire arena roared its disapproval at the priest.

The villain's face burned red. "Tutankhamun has failed you," he screamed into the brown haze. "He chose a child to fight for your freedom and his warrior brat has fallen!" He picked up his staff and flung it into the crowd. "Silence!" he demanded.

Then the priest felt something enormous fall upon his back. Before he was aware of it, he was lying face down on the arena floor. He drew his head from the sand and gasped for air. A terrible pain seized his body, a pain Ramose had never experienced during his time in the Land of the Living. As soon he managed to draw breath, he exhaled a shriek of agony. With great effort, he pushed himself on to his side just in time to see his attacker emerge from the dust cloud.

A golden bird stood before him, its feathers shimmering in the moonlight.

A thunderous cheer rose from the crowd.

As Ramose struggled to his feet, he saw that the bird was actually Jonas, clad in suit of golden armor. A pointy beak jutted from his helmet. The priest wheezed mocking laughter.

"A chicken?" Ramose croaked. "This is the bird of your vengeance, Tutankhamun?"

"No," Tut called from the stage. "It is the bird of Amun's justice."

Ramose raised his hand and a bolt of lightning flashed from his palm. The bolt struck Jonas, but this time he remained standing. The plates of his golden armor glowed and crackled with raw electric energy.

Ramose started. "Impossible!" he hissed. The priest let loose a barrage of bolts that all found their target, yet every one failed to harm Jonas. Instead, the bolts caused his armor to glow with increasing intensity.

Jonas could feel the energy coursing through him. He lunged forward with inhuman speed and laid into Ramose with terrific force. Each strike of his staff left the priest's armor dented and the body underneath bruised and broken. The villain cried out, flailing his arms as he attempted to stagger away.

"No fair!" he wheezed. "Slaves! Destroy the chicken!"

But the jackal-headed sentries remained still.

"Traitors!" he spat. Then a strange sound caught his attention. A buzzing and crackling echoed throughout the arena. Ramose turned to find arcs of electricity spreading into the air all around Jonas.

"Tell the Devourer that Fight-O McDuffins sent you!" Jonas said as he charged across the arena toward Ramose. When he jammed his staff into the sand, the pole bowed under his weight, then launched him into the Felonious Flip-Kick Whammy Buster. Jonas released the pole and began spinning sideways in the air. "Bock-bock chicken!" he yelled as his armored feet made contact with Ramose, hurling the villain backward.

Ramose smashed into the wall like a bullet, sending a dust plume into the air as the arena erupted into chants of "Bock-bock chicken!"

Jonas leaped to his feet and lifted his staff from the sand. He held it over his head and smiled.

The jackalheads on the platform were chanting along as they hoisted Tut on their shoulders. The boy-king waved his walking stick and smiled.

A huge crack formed and ran the length of the arena wall. Smaller breaks in the facade spread out and chunks began to break free and fall. Jonas watched in amazement as the pieces dissolved before touching the sand.

"Nooo!" Panicked cries rose from the stands.

Jonas scanned the crowd. Everyone in the audience was fading away. Jonas could see right through them. The chanting stopped as chaos erupted. Some people broke into pained wails while others cheered. Others leaped from their seats and attempted to escape, but no matter which way they ran, they continued to vanish like everyone else.

The jackalheads hurriedly placed Tut in the sand and scattered.

"Thank you!" Jonas heard someone say through the commotion.

He looked up and saw Edgar and Helen Aldrich standing at the arena wall.

"Thank you for freeing us, brave Chicken-Boy!" they called down.

"You're welcome!" he said as he waived.

"Bock-bock chicken!" Helen called.

"Bock-bock chicken!" Jonas echoed. Then he heard a voice behind him. He turned to find Tut alone on the platform.

"Thank you for your bravery, Champion, and farewell!" the king yelled. "Bock-bock chicken!"

"Bock-bock chicken!" Jonas called back.

19
BOCK-BOCK CHICKEN!

Sejal looked on as her father cradled Jonas's head in his hands while Mrs. Shurmann administered CPR.

"Come on," Dr. Hazari whispered, "breathe, Jonas, breathe."

Jonas's dad clutched Tallula's hand, as they both stood by, helplessly.

Everything seemed so unreal. It was like a bad dream that would vanish as soon as they all woke up. The only thing was, no one was waking up—including Jonas.

Sejal looked to Orville, who was standing at the base of the scaffolds with Jonas's white feathers still tied around his head. He was shouting up to CatBob and Neil, who were tiring from battling the slithering skeleton overhead.

"Okay," Orville called, "I'll ask." He turned back

to Sejal. "Anything yet?"

Sejal tried to swallow the lump in her throat, but it wouldn't go down. She shook her head.

Orville nodded and bit back his own tears before calling back to the felines in a cracking timbre. "He'll come around, guys," he said. "He's tough. He's gonna make it!"

High-pitched whines and hisses echoed through the atrium amid the constant sound of rattling. Cat-Bob and Neil had been leaping between the scaffold towers, doing their best to keep Arthur away from Jonas, but the rattling was getting closer and so were the skeleton's eerie blue flames.

"Just keep it busy for a few more minutes, boys!" Orville shouted. But he knew there was only so much the cats could do. They were tired and the dead never rest.

A flash of blue flame drew Orville's attention and he saw Arthur's tail strike Neil. The cyclopean feline cried out has he tumbled over the side of the scaffold.

Orville scrambled for his plummeting friend and managed to catch him before he hit the ground.

"I gotcha, Big Guy!" he huffed.

Neil reached out with his paw and tapped Orville on the face. "Thank you, Orville," he said.

A scream pealed through the darkness above.

Orville and Neil looked up and saw that CatBob had jumped onto the monster. The detective gripped its bones with his front claws and gnawed away as he delivered rabbit kicks with his hind feet. Arthur's top half twisted and began coiling around the peachy feline like a thick rope.

"No!" Orville shouted. "Get away from it, Bob—it's going to wrap itself around you."

But it was too late. Even as CatBob raked the delicate ribs away with deft swipes of his paws, the spine squeezed his body and held him fast. The detective cried for help, but he was out of Orville's reach.

"Hang on, CatBob!" Orville called as he hoisted himself up on one of the steel poles, "I'm coming!" He reached out for another, but stopped when a bright flash lit up the entire room.

All eyes looked up to the scaffold where CatBob squirmed in the coil of bones. Brilliant flashes of blue light strobed from the skull. The jaw-bone yawned open and an anguished scream resounded throughout the rafters.

Dr. Hazari felt something moving in his hands. He looked down and saw Jonas's chest was contracting. "He's alive!" Dr. Hazari yelled.

Everyone gathered around as Jonas sucked air into his lungs with sharp, convulsive gasps. Then his eyes shot open as he bolted upright and yelled,

"Bock-bock, chicken!"

The wailing overhead abruptly stopped and the bones froze in place. CatBob wiggled enough to loosen Arthur's grip, then leaped away just as the blue flames went out and the bones fell to the platform, scattering over the sides.

Orville crouched over Neil as a shower of bones rained down. Hundreds of vertebrae bounced from steel beams and wooden platforms before shattering into pieces on the atrium floor.

When the deluge stopped, Orville straightened up and looked around. "Way to go, Drumsticks!" he yelled. Then he felt something heavy land on his head and he screamed. "Help! It's got me!" He crouched down and began running in circles. "Get it off me!" he screamed as he flailed his arms in the air.

"Hold still!" Sejal cried as she raced over to help him.

A moment later Orville felt the weight lifted from his head. He pushed the feathers from his eyes and looked down at CatBob, who lay cradled in Sejal's arms.

"Jeez, Orville, it was only CatBob," she said.

The peachy feline smiled up at Orville. "Thanks for the landing pad," he said.

Orville scooped up Neil and motioned for Sejal to follow him to see Jonas.

Everyone was wiping away tears of joy as they watched Mrs. Shurmann shower her son with kisses.

"I'm okay, Mom," Jonas repeated to Mrs. Shurmann, who could not stop crying. He looked up at Sejal, Neil, Orville and CatBob and smiled. "I met King Tut and Edgar and Helen Aldrich!" he exclaimed. "They were trapped, but I saved them from a priest named Ramose II."

That's when the front doors burst open and a team of paramedics rushed in carrying black cases. They crowded around Jonas and went to work, asking him questions, taking his pulse, shining lights into his eyes, and examining his head. Within minutes, he was strapped to a gurney and loaded into an ambulance.

* * *

The doctors said that Jonas had suffered a serious concussion and he would be required to stay at the hospital for a few days while they ran tests. Although Jonas didn't like being stuck in the hospital, he did need the rest. After a couple of days spent sleeping, the nurse announced that he had visitors.

Jonas smiled when he heard chants of "Bock-bock chicken!" The curtain was yanked back to reveal Sejal, Dr. Hazari, Orville, and Tallula. Orville and Dr.

Hazari each held a plastic pet carrier.

"Hey, CB! We heard you were finally awake, so we came as soon as we could." Orville tossed a bulging shopping bag into Jonas's bed. "We even brought you a change of clothes."

Jonas leaped up, tore his feathers from the bag, and disappeared into the restroom. When he emerged, he found CatBob and Neil Higgins walking around on his bed, sniffing the sheets.

Neil examined him with his amber eye and sniffed his hand. "How are you feeling?" he asked.

"Okay," Jonas said. "But I think I'm having problems remembering things from that day. At least that's what the doctor said after I told him what I could remember."

"Well, everyone at school believes you," Sejal said. "People can't stop talking about how you, Cat-Bob, and Neil saved the school from a real-life monster."

"I don't remember that part." Jonas frowned. "I don't even remember going to school that day. I just remember what happened after I fell."

Everyone exchanged glances, and then leaned in.

"I know you guys won't believe me, but I met King Tut and Edgar and Helen Aldrich," Jonas said. "They were trapped in a city created by an evil priest of Aten named Ramose II."

Everyone was silent as they took in what Jonas had said. Then Dr. Hazari spoke up. "You may not be able to remember, but do you know what books you've read for your report on the Aldriches?"

"None," Jonas answered. "My dad bought me the book about Tut's treasure from the COSI gift shop but I never had the chance to read it."

Dr. Hazari nodded. "Have you ever heard of Ramose II before?"

"No," Jonas said. "But he was a bad guy. Tut said Ramose's father worked for his father and grandfather, but he wasn't like Ramose II. When Tut finally became Pharaoh, Tut's uncle Ay conspired with Ramose II. They murdered Tut because Ay wanted to remain king and Ramose wanted revenge on Tut for banning the cult of Aten."

Everyone looked at Dr. Hazari as he shook his head. "I see," he said.

"Is that true?" Orville asked.

Dr. Hazari raised his eyebrows and exhaled. "I have no idea. Only a few people could have known for sure if Tutankhamun was murdered, and all of them have been dead for thousands of years."

Jonas frowned and ran his hands down his partners' backs as they hugged his arms with their tails.

"I'm not saying you're wrong," Dr. Hazari added. "In fact, I'm fascinated that you know who Ramose

II was. Despite the fact that his father's tomb was one of the most well preserved crypts ever discovered, it's not known for certain if Ramose I had any children. And Tut's assassination has been suggested before by a few learned historians, but there has been no conclusive proof discovered to back up such a theory."

"Hey, at least we'll have a cool angle for our report, right?" Sejal chimed in.

"Yeah," Jonas agreed.

"That is, if we still have to finish our reports," Sejal added.

"What do you mean?"

"Well, no one has seen Edison since you fell." Sejal's eyes grew wide. "He disappeared right after and hasn't come back since. The police are actually looking for him."

"He was the shadow that left," Jonas whispered.

"So, did King Tut tell you if the ring was his?" Neil asked.

"He did!" Jonas shouted. "I almost forgot." He looked up at Sejal. "Tut's ring—the beetle ring—where is it?"

Sejal looked to her dad, who looked to Orville. "Your parents don't have it?" Sejal asked.

"I don't think so," Jonas said. "They never mentioned it."

"We found the ring's owner," Dr. Hazari put in. "Corwin Bachert, the man who loaned the skeletons for the COSI exhibit at school."

"Oh," Jonas mumbled. "It really did belong to King Tut."

"We know," Sejal said. "Corwin told us."

"He also told us it's cursed," Dr. Hazari added. "You should be happy it's gone. He said it's an evil thing."

Jonas looked away. "Not any more," he muttered under his breath.

20
FISH-GIRL RETURNS

Jonas's life slowly returned to normal in the weeks that followed. He was released from the hospital and didn't have to go to school for a whole two months—which he thought was great at first. But after the holiday break was over, he was forced to spend most of the time alone.

Although his dad worked from home, Mr. Shurmann was usually too busy to do anything fun and Jonas's mom worked late most days at her vet office. And even after Jonas begged to have CatBob and Neil stay over for a few days, he found they spent most of their time sleeping. They were cats, after all. His last hope was Orville, who did manage to host a few *SmashLord III* tournaments, but he and Tallula were busy trying to adopt out all of Orville's houseguests so the renovations of Castle Dusenbury could resume.

This made Sejal's visits the highlights of Jonas's week. She filled him in on all of the developments at school—including a report that the police had broken down the door to Edison's house and found the place totally empty.

"But it wasn't just empty," Sejal explained. "It was covered in dust, like no one had lived there in decades, except for a trail of footsteps where someone had been walking the same path every day. It led from the back door to the dining room, where there was a clean spot along one of the walls. Otherwise, there were no other footprints in the rest of the house. Oh! And the whole place smelled like Edison's farty cologne. Freaky, huh?"

"Super-freaky," Jonas said. "Where did you hear this?"

"My mom," Sejal replied. "She wasn't very happy with my dad and me for helping you, but she does love good gossip—and weirdo Edison Tomb is who everyone is talking about." She paused and gave a sly smile. "I even caught her bragging to some of the ladies at the salon that her daughter was there when it all happened—helping the Chicken-Boy.

"And I talked to Corwin Bachert," she added. "He said the police searched the school and they couldn't find the ring. They suspect Edison took it off your finger after you fell, then he just ran away. But Corwin said he was happy the ring was gone and felt sorry for whoever had it."

"Yeah, I guess," Jonas muttered.

"Anyway, Corwin said he will help us with our report," she said.

"We still have to do that?"

Sejal nodded. "We got a new substitute and she said, since everyone had been working on their reports, we might as well finish them."

Jonas got up, took some papers from his book bag, and handed them to Sejal.

"What's this?" she asked.

"My report."

"Jonas, you're not supposed to do any schoolwork while you recover."

"I didn't. I wrote it the night before my accident. You just reminded me." Jonas became very quiet, then turned away. "I'm sorry for being such a jerk, Sejal. And I'm really sorry for hitting you." His cheeks became flushed and tears sprang from his eyes.

"You weren't yourself," Sejal slid his report into her book bag. "But thank you. That apology makes me want to hit you back a lot less."

Jonas smiled weakly.

Sejal produced another packet from her bag and handed it to him.

"Oh, no thanks," Jonas said. "I'm not allowed to do homework, remember?"

Sejal smirked. "It's not homework. It's the new Fish-Girl and Meows story."

"Oh, great." Jonas rolled his eyes.

"Shut up," Sejal chided. "You'll like this one. Fish-Girl and Meows join forces with the Chicken-Boy of Clintonville and the Crime Cats. And so far, it's even more popular than the last one."

"All right," Jonas moaned as he eyed it reluctantly. "I'll have Neil read to me when he wakes up. But if we don't like it, we're going to let CatBob pee on it."

Sejal laughed. "That's fair," she said.

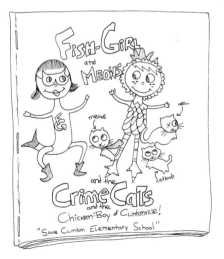

"CAT BATHS"

Healthy cats do their own grooming, but if your cat-friend gets into something sticky or smelly (or gets invited to a fancy dinner), you may have to give them a bath. And while you may get lucky and find your cat-friend likes taking a bath—like CatBob—the fact is that most cats don't. Here are some tips to make it go as smoothly as possible:

1. Bathe regularly. Bathe your cat-friend from a young age. If you give your cat-friend a bath a couple of times a year from when they are small, they will see bath time as a normal part of life. Some cats react badly simply because they aren't used to it.

2. Choose the time. Give your cat-friend a bath during the time of day that they are tired. Have a play session to tire them out before the bath is also a good idea.

3. Claws. Make sure you trim your cat-friend's claws before the bath, or have them done by your vet.

4. Brush beforehand. Brush your cat-friend's coat. There are many kinds of brushes on the market. Investing in a more expensive brush that effectively removes their undercoat will help keep your clothes and house cleaner and your cat-friend more comfortable.

5. Pair up. Although some cats are docile during bath time, not all are. You will have a better time if you have someone help you. Prepare to get wet!

6. Draw the bath. Place a rubber mat in the tub so your cat-friend doesn't slip and fall. Then draw a bath of lukewarm—not hot—water about 3 to 4 inches deep.

7. Soak. Wet your cat-friend down using an unbreakable plastic cup. Do not use anything made of glass, or anything heavy, in case the wet cup slips from your grasp and falls on your cat-friend.

8. Shampoo. Use shampoo specifically made for cats. Research cat shampoos, because not all are the same. Lather up your cat-friend's coat, working in the direction of the hair growth. Do not put shampoo on or in your cat-friend's ears, face, or eyes.

9. Rinse. Gently rinse the shampoo off with lukewarm water from your unbreakable plastic cup.

10. Use conditioner. If your cat-friend has long hair, you will need to use a conditioner or detangler for cats. Your groomer or vet can recommend one.

11. Wash their face. Usually a clean washcloth soaked in lukewarm water will clean your cat-friend's face. But if your cat-friend's face has gotten dirty, dilute some cat shampoo and gently wipe their face. Be very careful not to get any shampoo in their ears and/or eyes.

12. Dry. Once the shampoo residue is all off, remove your cat-friend from the water and towel-dry them from head to toe with a clean towel. Let their coat air dry in a warm, dry place, away from drafts. If the noise doesn't bother your cat-friend, you can dry their coat with a hairdryer on the lowest heat setting. If your cat-friend has long hair, you will have to separate tangles with a wide-toothed comb.

13. Treat. After bath time is over, reward your cat-friend with their favorite treat.

"FEEDING YOUR CAT-FRIEND"

Not all cats get invited to a fancy home-cooked dinner. And most people assume the cat food they find in the grocery store is good for their cat-friend because it is made for cats. Unfortunately, that's not always true. Here are some things to consider when selecting a food for your cat-friend:

1. No dog food. Never feed your cat-friend dog food. Feeding dog food to your cat can lead to the development of heart, eye, and neurological disease.

2. Food allergies. Cats have food allergies just like people. If your cat-friend is having problems with their food, it may be due to food allergies. A visit to your veterinarian can help in figuring out what foods are giving your cat-friend problems.

3. Protein. Cats need protein. That means they eat meat.

Never feed your cat-friend a vegetarian diet. Look on the ingredients list for chicken, turkey, lamb, salmon, etc., followed by named organs, e.g. chicken liver or chicken heart (both rich sources of taurine). If in doubt, ask your vet. They will know your cat-friend's medical history and will tell you what to look for.

4. No grains. Many cats are allergic to wheat and corn. Cornmeal is often used as filler in cheap food. Instead, look for better filler ingredients like green peas, sweet potatoes, or potato starch.

5. None of these either. Avoid foods that list "by-products," "meat and/or bone meal," "digest," or added sugars. Avoid chemical preservatives, including BHA, BHT, ethoxyquin, and propyl gallate.

6. Fat. Look for a named fat source on the ingredients list, like "chicken fat." You may also see sunflower oil or other oils in more expensive foods.

7. Taurine. Taurine is an amino acid that cats need to stay healthy. Scientists have found that if cats don't get enough taurine, they can develop retinal degeneration and/or heart disease. Make sure your cat-friend's food has taurine in it.

8. "Complete and balanced." Look for that phrase on the food you buy. Do not buy food that doesn't have that phrase on the packaging.

9. Servings. A healthy, active, 8-pound adult cat needs about 30 calories per pound per day. You can use that formula to figure out how many calories your cat-friend needs in a day. When you have calculated that number, divide it by two. The number you now have is the number of calories for each meal you serve. Never leave dry food out in a bowl for your cat-friend to eat as much of as they want, but always make sure they have fresh water. It's best to feed your cat-friend once in the morning and once in the mid-to-late afternoon.

10. Switching it up. Varying the brand and flavor of food will keep your cat-fried from getting sick of the same food every day.

Made in the USA
Middletown, DE
28 October 2016